Beach Duty

A Steamy Romance Holiday Collection

Sofia Aves

First Edition

Published by Little Quail Press

ISBN ebook 978-1-923471-89-4

Print 978-1-923471-10-8

Summer With A Ranger

A Texan Devils undercover summer fling

Hudson Wittington never thought he'd leave the LA Fire Dept. to cross the country and accept a trial position in an elite Texas Ranger's unit that includes undercover work in Tijuana. But that's where he finds himself when a beach babe decides to use him as her personal bodyguard to ward off undesirables for the remainder of his trip.

It should be an easy job–both of them. But before he heads back to Texas, Hudson learns a few home truths about himself, and he might have given away his heart to a woman he isn't sure wants to risk hers on him in the process.

Because sex on the beach isn't just a drink

CHAPTER ONE

HUSDON

One week into my job as the newest recruit in Rhys Archer's elite Texas Ranger Unit out of Austin and I was sitting on a beach in Tijuana, sipping cocktails decorated with pretty umbrellas and plastic red cherries.

Hudson Whittington, Texas Ranger.

Who would have thought it?

It wasn't a bad way to start a new job, if I didn't say so myself. Not only did I pull undercover work as my first assignment, but I also got to wrangle the floating eye candy tourist population for a solid seven days.

My first wasn't a long assignment, but I knew the gig for what it was: a test.

Make contact, get the product, and swan around for a full week. Don't trip yourself up, and don't break your cover. Come back home when you're done.

Those were the rules I was given to earn a shiny brass star and a white hat. My sandbox to play in. Do the job, and do it well, or haul my ass back to California where I spent the last nine years as a fixture in the LA Fire Department.

I'd never had a problem with my career choices and I loved my job, but now that Archer had given me a taste of what I could do on this side of the border, I wasn't sure I could go back.

Which made this a pass/fail task with an ultimatum at the other end. It was kind of easier, to be fair.

And three days into my allocated time on the beach, I was halfway there. I made the contact, tasted drugs for the second time in my life—the first time during college and I fucking hated the lack of control over my body and thoughts—and made a faux friend for life in my Tijuana dealer, Tag. The name had a ... nice ring to it. I was scheduled to pick up the product I was supposed to pretend to distribute back home in Cali in a few days, then head home.

Only if I had my way, I wasn't going back to

Cali. Austin, Texas, would be my new/old-to-me baseline. The dirt I grew up tasting.

Memories of my childhood attempted to flood back: the house I used to live in, the family that fell apart. That was how I ended up on a different side of the country. My chest closed at the emotional deluge I rejected on sight, and I sucked in a long, slow breath.

Not the time. Or the place.

Because right now I had a date with a beach.

I sank into the divot my body made in my borrowed beach towel, the sand accommodating my mass gracefully, heating my back in the sun-warmed sand. It wasn't midday yet, and the extra endorphins already flooded my body. Being a Texas Ranger might not be like this every day, but right now, I'd take it.

Of course, the singular doubt in my gut remained that maybe I wasn't as worthy as Archer thought.

Walking into his office was the singularly most nerve wracking thing I'd ever done. The quiet man with rust coloured hair and a scarred face stared across the desk at me while I tried not to fidget like a teenage kid called in to see the principal.

I'd always been proud of being a firefighter, but that career choice seemed flimsy the moment I walked into the Austin unit's office. The space was filled with men in pressed shirts and white hats, that little star badge displayed somewhere on their person.

Dressed in faded jeans, boots I did up at the entrance foyer, and an old gray LA Fire Dept. tee, I stood out in the worst of ways.

Not that I felt lesser in any physical sense; I was more than a match for the team in terms of muscle and height, but ego wise... I was born and bred in Texas and made the move to LA chasing sun and surf.

And a little excitement.

Those career choices got me laid, paid and in front of Archer, or at least that was what he told me. How he picked me out of the population of previous and current Texan residents I couldn't say, only that I was grateful for the chance.

That, and my intention not to fuck up.

That seed of doubt dissipated with a fine spray of sand and salt water dripping on me. I cracked one eye open to find a visage of tanned and toned skin in a sapphire blue bikini standing before me in a sarong. One muscular thigh slipped out from beneath the gold and blue filmy material.

The girl perched on her towel she placed right

beside me, closer than any stranger should be, drop dead stunning or not. My stomach tensed, and not by design, just from her proximity. One slim arm reached out behind her. She arched her back slightly with one leg bent, and the other straight out as she looked down at the imperiously.

"You're my bodyguard for the next four days."

"I'm your what?" I raised both eyebrows and tried not to waggle them, but holy *shit* on a beach ball was she gorgeous. "I didn't know they made them like you in Tijuana."

She smirked, nary a giggle in sight, flicking beachy blonde waves over her shoulder. Everything about this woman was hard, in a goddess sort of way. From the set of her mouth to the fiery blaze behind deep blue eyes, her straight spine, the way she sat... everything was utter perfection to my eyes.

Except maybe that golden hair that reminded me of California.

In one fell swoop I was home sick.

Setting my teeth, I flexed both arms, tucking them behind my head and closed my eyes. I couldn't work out what was hotter: her gaze, or the sun.

"I've got a deadline, and I need protection from this." Her tone bordered on derisive. I kept my eyes closed but imagined her waving a hand at the remainder of the population on the beach. "You'll stop them from hitting on me."

"What makes you think anyone wants to hit on you?" I was glad my eyes stayed shut. After that snappy little repartee, I fully expected a slap in the face.

Sand flicked on my stomach, and I managed not to flinch. *Just.*

"Asshole," she said idly. "What's your name?"

"Hudson. Whittington." I managed around a thick tongue that didn't' feel like it belonged in my mouth, and cracked an eye open.

"Skye Gallagher." She held out a hand, complete with callouses, and short, French polished tips.

The best of both worlds. A Queen, if rough at a few hidden edges. I liked what I saw already, though I knew she'd be a ballbuster. Knowing she worked with her hands sometimes, even if it was sport or around the yard, lit something inside me. I wanted to see her sweat. I wanted to see her get filthy and lick her clean.

Where they fuck did that come from?

I had a job to do, for fuck's sake. But still, a little eye candy and a summer fantasy could be fun to indulge in. Plus, her proposition fit my cover. *Yeah. That works.*

I pulled my head out of my cock and bullshit long enough to respond to her.

"That's apt."

"How's that?" She stared at me imperiously through narrowed, slitted eyes.

"Gallagher. It means *stranger*. Or warrior. Depends which side of the internet you believe."

"How do you know that?"

"I grew up living next door to some Gallaghers. Good neighbors."

"Funny, that." Her eyes softened, the tiniest bit, or maybe I imagined it. "Now stay, Huddy boy, and look pretty."

Who said I was staying?

But we both knew I would. I kept the wince off my face at the shitty nickname all the same.

"Yes, ma'am."

After that she stayed silent while my mind wandered. I was halfway through a damn fine daydream about toned thighs and a blue bikini that matched her blue eyes when a finger poked me in the ribs.

"Wake up, baby oil boy. You're turning lobster red."

"I am?" I cracked open an eye and looked down at my chest, spotting nothing but a bronzed plateau that matched hers, albeit with less curves. "I don't see what you're seeing."

"Clearly not." That smirk was back in her voice.

"So, I'm your bodyguard." I mean, who was I to say no to a pretty woman? Besides, my job was to stay low. Look like an overgrown kid out for fun and sun and maybe a few drugs. The thought of her believing that story hit me square in the guts, and I pushed it aside. "Who says we're staying the same length of time?"

"I'm here for a few days. Not sure." Skye shifted beside me as I raised up onto my elbows, cracking my neck. She winced. "Ouch."

"Yeah, that wasn't the best." I rubbed the back of my neck. "Where are you staying?" She rattled off the name of the quaint little beach cottage Archer booked for me, a word I hadn't been able to pronounce since I arrived. "Oh, good. We're staying in the same place," I said dryly.

The tiny little cottage had eight rooms, each seemingly smaller than the last, but it was cute, across the road from the beach, and it was two doors up from my new bestie, Tag the mini drug lord.

"Perfect." She smiled, and her face lit up in a whole new way. "Staying till Sunday?"

"Yeah." I pretended not to be floored but might have drooled on her a little.

Damn, a girl with her own mind, knowing what she wanted and who looked like that? Ticked all my boxes, straight up.

Still, I was supposed to be working. Four days I was going to be paired with this girl? I mean, I could haul my ass off the beach and leave her to it any time. She wasn't quite the type of damsel in distress I was used to rescuing. But seeing as I had some spare time...

"I do have shit to do here, you know."

"I'll be fine while you do your manly stuff. Anyway, baby oil boy, or whatever you use. You're gonna look like a lobster by dinner."

"Yes, ma'am," I said resignedly, hiding my own smirk, thinking back on her introduction. "What's your deadline for?"

"Creative nonfiction."

What the fuck is that?

She raised an eyebrow. "Eloquent. Maybe you can be my test subject."

"I– what?" I shook my head, rubbing sunscreen on my face and the rest of me.

Her azure gaze tracked an appreciative line down my body that stirred my blood. I returned the favor, leaving my attention to wander over her toned calves and stomach with that sexy goddamn line down the middle. The girl put some serious hours into working her body beautifully for her to look like that. I was just there to appreciate it.

"You really don't have a filter, do you?" She laughed at me, bringing me back.

Golden waves settled almost to her waist in long, oversized curls, looking natural as hell. Actually, everything about her looked natural, which was a bit of a relief. Living in LA meant there was a whole lot of fake going on, and I'd never been able to stomach it. Tits with implants just didn't feel right in my hands.

She laughed outright, and my mouth snapped shut.

I gave her a crooked smile. "Nope. No filtered fucks served here."

"Good. Maybe you can call me out with my bull-shit if it gets too much."

I raised both eyebrows. She seemed real about it, but who knew. Maybe I'd get to test that out some time. Four days with this girl and we'd be driving each other fucking nuts. She clearly a profes-sional of whatever creativeness she delved into. I was more the laid back sort, happy with my ass in the sand and making sure everyone around me was safe.

Still, she was sexy as hell, and I did have time on my hands.

"I can do that," I hedged, wondering what the hell I just signed up for.

I straightened, wrapping my arms around my knees and looked out over the water. The glorious morning merged into an afternoon filled with dark clouds across the horizon. Tendrils of out of season fog preceding the oncoming storm crept across the water.

"Looks like you want to pack that up, princess." The last rays of sun soaked my back with glorious heat. *Here's hoping for more assignments over the border.* "So, what's this creative thing?" I scratched my brow, trying to remember what she said.

Skye jerked, staring at the encroaching wall of water, and I didn't mean the surf sort. "Shit." The girl swore liberally as she packed her things, earning a few glances from other beachgoers as they collected their belongings, trudging back up the still-warm sand.

"Walk you back to the cottage? I think we're staying at the same place." I repeated myself as I folded my towel and stuffed one hand into my pocket.

"Thanks." Not beating around the bush, she swung an oversized beach tote onto her shoulder with everything stuffed inside, including a pale pink laptop case decorated with gold swirls all over it.

"Cute." I offered her an easy smile. I hoped. When she shot me a raised eyebrow and a disapproving look, I waved a hand feebly at her bag. "Laptop case. It's pretty."

Great grasp on the English language right there.

"No filter, and not smooth. Glad you've got muscles going for you, big boy." She tapped my shoulder and strode ahead of me. Each step was sure in the sand, her toned calf muscles tensing with each step as she plowed her way toward the street.

"Maybe a heart to match," I murmured to her back.

I kept my eyes fixed straight ahead and rolled my shoulders. Welp. At least the last few days of my trip wouldn't be wasted. I could perfect some of that lacking charm that the rest of the unit had going on before I walked back in the door and claimed my badge on Monday.

Keeping my eyes fixed firmly ahead I couldn't

help my gaze wandering towards the perfect pair of hips that swayed gently as she walked.

Okay, so I lied to myself earlier. Not everything was hard about her.

CHAPTER TWO

HUDSON

"You'll get your product." Tag, the Mexican dealer contact Archer sent me to find nodded, his arms folded over his chest. "When I can confirm who you are from California. Got a few connections there I might check in with, seeing as you're new blood to the area and all." Sweat glistened on his pock-marked face as he leered at me.

I tried not to look at the sores decorating his skin, or the decay in his mouth when he offered me a too-wide smile and an expulsion of tepid air.

My stomach turned as I eyed the plethora of designer drugs laid out on the folding table in several assorted baggies, trying not to belay my disquiet. *Here's hoping Archer's got someone good on the other side of the country.* Because if the dude looked me up, he'd find a fairly clean man with no criminal history and no trust factor, leaving me a buck shy of the drugs I was meant to take back to Texas.

"Take your time." I leaned against the doorway, scratching my shoulders on the hard ridge, and tried not to panic.

Breathe. Archer wouldn't have sent you in if he didn't have faith in you.

Or backed me up. Unless there was an initiation ceremony I missed.

A slightly smaller man with dark hair perched at the other end of the short table counting money and drinking straight from the tequila bottle at his side. The man had a barrel chest that looked like he could cripple a bear with a one-armed stranglehold.

"Got some friends in SoCal, we do." Tag turned to the man counting his money. "Don't we, Angel?"

Angel nodded, not raising his head from his counting and scribbling something on a pad beside him. I took in as much detail about the room as I possibly could. What sort of weapons they both carried, the size of the stacks of bills on the table, and the number of drugs in their possession.

I knew narcotics tracking was a huge part of Archer's unit and prevented them from entering the

US. That and human trafficking seemed to be his main focus from the short rundown I got in his office.

That was five days ago, and it suddenly seemed like months.

Angel offered me the tequila. I took the bottle with some small reservations, wiping the lip with my shirt and slugged two solid mouthfuls before handing it back. The Patrón burned its way down my throat and numbed my lips.

Angel didn't so much as look up as I handed the bottle back, but I could swear the man smiled.

"So, who you gonna call?" I lifted my lips at my own joke, though Tag looked at me curiously. I shook my head. "It doesn't matter. I'm heading back in a few days. Had a long damn night." I tacked on the information that wasn't entirely false.

I spent the night watching the storm roll through and a pair of long legs that appeared over my veranda at the back of the cottage, the sounds of the beach filtering through the still night. Turned out my beach babe took the room next to mine. She had perfect toes and perfect feet too, setting off a fetish I didn't know I had until then.

Skye. I discovered her name on my second day on bodyguard duty at the beach. Not that she said much to me since then. My time in this shithole of a building was almost up, and I was determined to at least get myself a decent kiss from the girl, refusing to leave Tijuana without one.

I inclined my head, trying to focus back on my job and not perky tits and pink painted toenails that matched her laptop case.

Fuck me. Or her. Either way, I was good with it.

I shifted discreetly to adjust my reaction to the thought. "Anyway. Let me know if you want me to take anything back, or when I head back next time I'm down."

Tag looked at me sharply. "You said take your time."

I shrugged again. "You can take all the time you want. This trip, next trip, whatever. I ain't going anywhere."

"Except back to SoCal," Angel broke his silence.

I nodded. "Except for that."

Tag folded his arms, his fingers jittering against his ribs. A side effect of using his own drugs? "Come back tomorrow," he said finally.

"Yes, ma'am." I ducked out the door before he realized what I said.

As I whipped out of the building, I could've sworn Angel smiled again.

* * *

I shouldn't have asked to read what she wrote.

That was all that crossed my mind as I stared down at the sexist gibberish that covered the digital page. Mind, seeing as she used a stranger to keep her single status card intact, I shouldn't have been surprised. Still, those words actually did reduce her sex appeal.

Minutely, maybe.

Fuck it. I still wanted that kiss.

Girls, if you're going to free air the kitty to encourage your man into action, he might need a little help. Flick the skirt, grind, let his hand wander. Sometimes men can be so ingrained in their habits they usually can't see what's right in front of them. But keep it discreet. Subtle is sexy.

I blinked at the screen. What were we, men from the stone ages? Miss Skye Hamilton–I stalked her name and maybe her number in the cottage guest book– needed a little nudge in the right direction. Setting my jaw, I handed her laptop back, ready to rain hell on her thoughts about my sex.

"You might wanna go easy on the, uh, aggressive

tone," I murmured, trying to work out how not to offend her while still getting my point across.

"You don't like men being objectified the way you have with women for centuries?" She tossed her glorious mane over her shoulder, a defiant glint in her eye that may or may not have bordered on maniacal.

"Damn, that's pretty. Huh?" I half reached out to touch her, though my hand suddenly stung like hell. "I didn't deserve that." I looked at her after studying the pink finger marks on the back of my hand. *Really* looked at her, and reassessed my original vision of the girl who wouldn't leave me alone.

Strong, but fragile underneath. She's covering cracks in her self-belief with muscle so she can fight what—who—ever comes at her.

Nothing about my epiphany made her less sexy in my eyes. Maybe more so, because now I knew she wasn't just driven, she was also a fighter.

"You did."

"Nope. Just stating what I see, princess."

"See." She flicked sand at me. The golden grains bounced off her laptop case. "Objectifying me."

"Yeah, just like you did the first day you planted your tush beside me—unobjectified tush—" I held up a finger when her pretty mouth opened—the objecti-

fied, pretty mouth I wanted to do bad, bad things to–
and kept talking. "–and called me baby oil boy, and
big boy, saying I had nothing going for me but
muscles." Okay, so I paraphrased, but that was the
gist of it.

Her mouth opened, and closed, then opened
again. "That's not–"

"What you meant to say, but it is what
happened," I reminded her gently. "Maybe you
should look inside with this one, Skye, before you
send that off to wherever it's going."

Personal blog, her friends group, a magazine,
what the fuck ever. But she'd get blasted for it, or I
had no faith in the female population standing up for
their favorite boy toys, and not the battery operated
sort.

"How dare you." She crossed her arms over her
chest. "Do you understand why I word things the
way I do?"

"Enlighten me."

"You're ridiculously white," she seethed. I raised
an eyebrow and gestured at her Aryan look. She
ignored me. "*Privileged* may as well be stamped
across your forehead. Or maybe it's on the back of
your designer polo."

"You're wearing the same label as me." I pointed

out, unwilling to back down just because her bikini bottoms got in a sexy, damp little twist.

"Hudson, let me mansplain this one for you." She ran her fingers through her hair. "I reach women in all corners of the US, and some farther afield. Some are very quiet, conservative areas. Some aren't white areas." The obsessive–excuse me, *passionate*–gleam replaced a flicker of exhaustion in her gaze, lifting the color in her face. "Let's say we went out on a date. We got along well, shared a hot kiss, and decided to take it further. Both of us being professional city dwellers, or wherever you come from. Would you think less of me in the morning for it?"

How long were you up writing for last night, Skye? Because she sure as hell outlasted me when I dozed in my chair for half the night, creating new fantasies about my beach towel buddy.

Her gaze fixed on me, and a flush travelled up my cheeks. I resisted the urge to curve my hand around her nape, pull her into me, and find out just what that scenario she outlined felt like first hand.

"Of course not."

The image of kissing her hard enough to push her against a wall in my room and run my hands up those toned thighs and beneath her sarong ripped through my mind on a swift current of searing arousal.

My cheeks weren't the only things overheating.

"Good." She smiled, and there was heat in her gaze, too. "Let's go back to those country areas. If those women suddenly did a lap dance for their very conservative partner, they could be labelled as sluts, abused, or thrown out. Certainly some would become homeless or humiliated. Maybe..." Her smile faded but her gaze remained intense. She didn't finish her sentence, and she didn't need to.

Point made.

I clenched my teeth. "I get that. But it's–"

"You do. Really?"

"Really, Skye. I do. It's making a man feel so objectified reading those words. The language. Where's the love and attraction between your couple in that scenario?" I searched her face this time, my palms pressed to my board shorts. Designer, sure. But only because they came from the closest shop in Texas when I was offered the job on a time trial basis.

"Oh. My. You are, aren't you?" She shot me a false eye roll and a snarky little smirk I wanted to kiss right off her face. "You're a romantic. For fuck's sake, Hudson. Grow up. The world is here for what we take, to make us feel better for our shortcomings. Let me assure you no woman will be happy with everything you do. Love doesn't work that way." Her short speech ended on a decisively bitter tang.

I pushed her laptop aside on her tote, leaned forward, and braced an arm over her head on her towel, forcing her to lean back or end up pressed chest to chest with me. Close enough to breathe in her lilies and dewdrops scent. Romantic? Hell, yes. I was a tragic, and I'd cling to that and my man card on my way to hell or my grave one day, whichever came first. No way was I stopping just because...

Skye stared at me through hooded eyes half-covered by thick lashes I wanted to brush my mouth over, and breathe her in. The need in me was reflected in her mirrored gaze. In her dilated pupils. But there was something more there...deeper than desire, something a little darker...

I swore inside my head, and touched her lips tenderly with aching fingers, wishing I'd figured her out that much sooner. Taken a risk that much sooner. "Who hurt you so bad you can't wear rose tinted glasses for a single moment, Skye?" I brushed my fingers over her cheek, guiding a stray golden strand behind her ear.

She squeaked, and pressed her hands to my

chest, though she didn't push me away. At all. "Don't touch me. Those things aren't real, Hudson." She slipped out from under me, already packing her things into her beach tote, her hands busy as she talked.

Hiding.

She shot me a fragile look, both filled with anger that I'd uncovered her secret and something...more, right before she took off across the beach, her sandals dangling from her fingers and spraying sand everywhere.

My chest closed again. *I shouldn't have said anything.* Should I? Fuck, I had no idea. But I couldn't leave her hurting like that, not when I was the one responsible for upsetting her.

Yeah, that sounded as good a reason as any.

I grabbed my towel, and something hit my foot. Something sharp with metal edges. I collected her purse, tucking the overfilled thing with cards and change and a star necklace poking out at all angles from it, and chased her across the road, darting between pedestrians and finally catching her in the hallway of the cottage.

"Damn, you move fast," I huffed, not really out of breath but startled she nearly out ran me. I got no answer as she shoved her door–*her unlocked door, what the actual fuck?*—open with trembling hands.

Taking the risk I probably shouldn't, I followed her in, closing and locking her door behind me. "Skye, I'm–"

"You shouldn't be in here." She stared at me with a blank face, all the roiling emotion of a moment before completely gone.

I blinked at her. Angry Skye, I could manage, even if she irritated the shit out of me. Derisive, snobby Skye, even fragile Skye. But blank Skye? Nope. Seeing her close off like that broke something inside me.

Swallowing hard, I held out her purse. "You left this."

She stared at me for a second, then caught the pink thing that matched her laptop case. Cursing myself internally as an utter asshole I let her take it, using the movement to circle her wrist in my hand loosely, stopping her retreat.

"Wait."

"No."

My eyes shut and I let her go.

Silence fell in the room.

"Just like that?" Her voice trembled a little.

I opened my eyes. "Just like that."

"You won't fight for what you want?" Blue eyes bored into mine like she could pierce my fucking soul.

"I'll never force a woman," I corrected her, my voice straining. My hands fisted at my sides, and I turned away from her. "Be safe, Skye."

"You're all the things I didn't write about." Surprise filled her voice.

Rolling my lips together, I squeezed them hard, and turned back. *Keep on walking, Hudson. Right out her door.* Naturally, I ignored that wise little voice. Why break a lifetime habit?

"Yeah, you're not writing about men like me. The ones with hearts, whether they wear them on their sleeves, or hide them away for that special life partner who respects them." I took a step closer, and she didn't move. "The men who revere their woman, who don't want anything more than to come home, spend time with her, and make sure her day wasn't a shit fight, even if his was. To give her everything." My voice cracked and I gave a hollow laugh, still closing the distance between us step by step. "You're right. I am a hopeless romantic. Maybe someday it will pay off."

"You mean it, don't you?" she whispered, that blank facade coming down, along with the fragile one I recognized. Underneath she was...raw. Beautiful. "You wouldn't hurt anyone by cheating or abuse."

I shook my head, unlocking my jaw painfully. "Fucking never."

A sound rose in her throat and in that second I knew exactly what happened to give her this fractured view of the world. She whirled on her heel, darting for the only other place she could run to hide in–the bathroom.

"You wanna know what a good man looks like, Skye?" I caught her swiftly and turned her into the circle of my arms, drawing her to my chest. "A good man protects. A good man knows when the boundaries have been crossed." I released her, watching her lips part as furious breaths panted past them. "But despite that, a good man will stay."

Stepping back, I kept an eye on her, ready to catch her if she–hell, after that I wasn't ready to say she might swoon but...yeah.

Swoon would fit.

CHAPTER THREE

HUDSON

"Filter, remember?" she murmured, her breaths slowing. "Why do you have to be so damn perfect?" Her sigh was long, hard, and heartfelt.

My chest ached for her. "I'm far from perfect, Skye. But I'll try to make up for the asshole who carved fear in your heart."

"Humble too, huh?" She shook her head, scraping her hands through her hair and pushing it back off her face. "Maybe you should be the ones writing the articles."

"That'd be a fun column." I smirked. "The world

according to Hudson. Yeah, I can see that being used as toilet paper."

Her smile softened. "You have no idea how powerful those words were to hear, do you?"

"Just a California boy on a beach trip." I shrugged, rubbing the back of my neck.

Her lilies and dewdrops scent wafted around me, filling my head with images of lazy afternoons in the cottage, kissing her until our mouths were puffy with it, and feeding her. That was a different fantasy all on its own. Fuck, just being near her was intoxicating. I couldn't imagine being this close to her full time. I'd never get an inch of work done, she was that damn distracting.

"Is that all?" She bit her lip, closing the distance between us, her lashes fluttering as she looked up at me and away a little too fast.

I caught her chin in my fingers, gently directing her gaze back to meet mine. "Yeah." My mouth dried on the lie. The partial lie. *I have to get fucking past this.* "I'm not that deep, beach girl. Just a guy having downtime."

"And what about the shady as fuck little shop you disappeared into yesterday? You came out smelling like pot and...other stale substances." Her nose wrinkled.

I barked a sharp laugh. "Gonna dig into all my secrets, princess?" I backed her into the wall, bracing my hands either side of her head, my arms at full extension to keep some semblance of distance, even if it was a shitty facade.

"Maybe?" She had the balls to toss her hair. Silky strands wrapped around my forearms, slithering over my skin like she'd just run her fingers along me.

I found it damn hard to breathe.

"Then dig, but don't be shocked when I wanna do a little exposing of my own." I dropped a hand to trace her ribs, resting my knuckles lightly against the sweet curve of her hip. If I wrapped my hand around her, she'd be wearing nothing in a short period and I wasn't about to break my promise to her–I wouldn't force her or put her on the spot so bad she felt like she had to choose something she didn't want.

Yeah, I was that kind of soppy romantic ass.

I shouldn't have worried.

Her hands pressed to my abs in answer, sliding up–thankfully, as my grasp on my control frayed–to rest on my chest. "Who are you, Hudson Whittington?" she breathed.

"Just a guy…" I leaned down and pressed my mouth over hers.

So much for resolve. Or not getting involved.

Fuck it. I need to taste her.

Her lips parted on a gasp as if she wasn't sure I'd take it that far and actually kiss her. I brushed my tongue across the gap between her lips, touching to hers, and I was fucked. All over.

Threading my hands through her gloriously soft hair, I plunged my tongue into her mouth in a dominating dance to glide along hers. A soft, throaty noise whispered between us, and suddenly mine weren't the only hands wandering.

Her nails scraped my shoulders lightly, and she tugged my hair, opening to me fully. I groaned into her mouth, running my palms the length of her body and cupping her ass to tuck her into me. She fit perfectly against me in every way. My knuckles grazed the wall, righting my sense of geography that skewed as I sank against her, grinding her body with mine. The soft little sounds she elicited riled me until we were a mess of roaming hands and wet mouths exploring each other.

Two days of teasing was enough to break both of us, apparently.

Swinging her up onto my hips, I tucked her ankles around me and backed up to the bed. The mattress butted the back of my knees, and I let us fall, with her on top.

Skye's squeak did the best things to my body. I pushed her down onto my erection, rubbing her bikini clad pussy over my length until I swore I'd burst in my pants. When she broke the kiss, slithering down my body to mouth my cock through my shorts, I nearly did.

Tangling my hands in her hair, I let her play, teasing me through the material with her tongue while figuring out how to free my cock with her hands while her mouth was busy. I breathed through my nose hard, levering up to watch her play as she managed to expose my skin to the warm Tijuana air, and lapped at my cock.

"Fuck, Skye," I whispered, fisting her hair gently, and let her have control.

"Yes, please." She gave me an impish grin that shot pure lust through my veins.

Her mouth did wonderful things, teasing and torturing me until I had to pull her up my body or paint her face with my name.

"Come up to me, princess. Right here." I patted my chest as she kneeled over me, her sapphire eyes glowing. Playing with the strings on her bikini, I traced my fingers along her covered skin like she'd teased me until a little wet spot formed and her breaths came too fast. "Nu uh. I want that cream in my mouth." I tucked my hands around the backs of her thighs and drew her over my face.

"Are you sure," she whispered, staring down at me.

"I'll never lie to you, Skye." *Except about who I am. Fuck.* That twinged, but I managed to keep my resistance off my face. I hoped. "Hands here." Capturing her wrists in a gentle hold, I guided them over my head to the bed frame, linking her fingers around the cool metal bar. "Don't let go until I spank this perfect ass. You got it?"

"Got it," she breathed, her hair tumbling over her face to almost hide her eyes that took in *everything*.

When was the last time this girl was loved, for fuck's sake? She was due for more than a little TLC. I got that her sharp edges and hard outlook might scare off a lesser man, but fuck it. That was his loss.

Cupping her ass I went to town, licking her sweetly, nipping and sucking until I learned the rhythm that did it for her, and which spots earned me the best sounds. Her thighs trembled around my head, and I knew I'd never forget the vision of her head flung back, screaming her orgasm as she came on my face.

Or the sweet, addictive taste of her.

No way in hell did I want to let this girl go, lies and work be damned.

Her legs trembled as I dived back in, managing to time my spanks with the crest of her second wave. Skye slumped forward, moaning over me. I tipped her gently sideways, angling her to slide along my body, both of us covered with a sheen of sweat and salt that allowed her to slither along my chest.

"Baby. Skye," I murmured, kissing her gently as she fell bonelessly into my arms, rolling on top of her body. "I need a condom if you have one." If she didn't...shit. It'd be a ten second nudie dash back to my own room while I prayed she hadn't changed her mind.

"Huh?" She blinked at me dozily, so cute and flushed I kissed her again and again until our bodies ground together in a slow rhythm designed to last hours.

"Condom, princess. Or I'll get something." I half rose on my elbows, but she pulled me back.

"Don't go anywhere," she murmured in that breathy voice that drove me crazy. "In my bag. That one. Blue. That– yes. Pocket." She managed one word guidance as I scrounged and found the crinkled foil that made me a happy man.

I ripped the pack open and rolled the condom

on, playing with her creamy pussy with my other hand. "Ready enough for me, princess?"

Her fingers grazed my length, and she spread her legs wide, hooking one knee over my hip and pushing her heel into my ass, driving me forward. "God, yes," she sighed.

Her head tipped back as I rubbed against her, then notched at her entrance, pushing inside. Heat enveloped me in a tight ring, leaving me breathing hard.

"Fuck, you're tight." I groaned, hanging my head down as she wiggled around me.

"Deeper," she demanded.

I slammed a hand to her hip, inching my way inside her, but unable to control myself with that sort of pretty little ass wiggle going on.

Skye gasped, her eyes flaring wide. "You said..."

"I said a lot of things, princess, and I can make love like any man, but I've also wanted to fuck you since you first threw your towel down next to mine on the beach." I slammed home, her cry and the way she strangled my cock with her pretty slicked pussy rocking me deeper, just like she begged. "Wish granted." I bottomed out, stroking her hair back from her face as I stilled. "You okay, Skye?" I pulled her out of her reverie somewhat.

"Yeah," she whispered, shuddering a little. "Go slow and– and deep for a second." Her eyelashes fluttered, mirroring the way she clamped down on me.

My instinct was to screw her hard and fast, but the girl knew what she wanted, and I was only starting to learn what she needed. Rocking deeper into her, I cupped the back of her head, holding our mouths together so we shared each frantic breath, pushing deeper into her like she asked.

Maybe a little rougher.

Her hands gripping my shoulders, she leveraged herself against me, meeting every thrust, both legs wrapped around me. Her first cry lit my soul on fire as she fucked herself on me, and when she faltered, I took over, driving deeper and not stopping, not even when she cried out, shivering in my arms. Damp strands clung to her face. I swept them out of the way so I could lick her throat, sucking and nibbling.

"Perfect, so fucking perfect." I soothed her with gentle kisses, slowing a little as she gazed up at me like I was nothing she'd ever seen before. "Don't let anyone ever tell you otherwise."

I kissed her long and slow, matching my thrusts to the rhythm we set together, showing her what beach love should feel like.

Skye came for me twice more before my spine tingled, signaling the end of my front row seat to watch her shatter around me again and again.

"So beautiful," I murmured, kissing her as I drove into her harder.

Skye's body tensed, and, already recognizing her reaction, I dug my fingers into her ass cheeks and slammed myself home, bellowing my release that mingled with hers.

I dropped my head to her shoulder and gathered her into my arms, the ocean lapping the shore outside the only sound that intruded on our peace.

CHAPTER FOUR

HUDSON

"It looks good." I tallied up the collection of baggies in my possession filled with thousands of dollars of street value and held out my hand. "Be back next month."

Tag shook greasily, and I wished I hadn't extended the favor.

"You'll be back faster than that," Angel huffed from his accounting pile. "Shit sells faster than fresh buds."

"Whatever." I breathed slow, controlled, and hopefully not too deep. *Nearly done.*

All that was left was to head back to Texas without being arrested, though I got the impression from Archer that the badge in my glove compartment would cover my ass back across the border.

That was all I had to achieve... that, and say goodbye to Skye.

I left her in her bed before I crawled back to my room and changed, trying to get my head around the job and out of her pussy. Because that's where my mouth had been when I realized I needed to move my ass. Waiting for her orgasm to crest, I licked her soothingly, tonging her swollen pussy lips from our frantic fuck sessions the night before.

Neither of us got much sleep, and I didn't relish pulling an all nighter in time to haul my ass in front of Archer first thing tomorrow. I wouldn't look fresh, but that was another thing I got about him. In this sort of job I didn't need to be, at least not first thing or the job I was sent to do wasn't done right.

"Thanks, man," I said to no one, tucking the baggies into my jeans and shooting a wave over my shoulder.

No one objected to my leaving, so I figured Agel would probably pocket the extra two hundred in the stacks later without telling his boss of the little bonus.

It was good to have a man in your pocket on the

other side, especially when part of me wondered that I wouldn't be sent back across the border if I earned that badge the way I hoped.

I slipped back into my room and found Skye sitting on my bed. "What are you doing in here?" My words came out harsh and I winced. "Sorry, I was..."

"Doing man shit. I remember." She looked at me through a curtain of glossy blonde waves. "And I remember falling asleep after you made me come, and eating my breakfast alone." She pouted, taking the sting out of her words.

I exhaled through my nose. "Yeah. Sorry about that." I headed for my luggage and knew there was no way she wasn't going to see the drugs I had to take back to fulfill my agreement with Archer. To prove my worth.

Shit.

"You wanna go get something else? Coffees? My treat." I offered, pulling cash out of my pocket.

She eyed the wad and shook her head. "Nope. I'm all packed and ready to go. Just gotta find a bus that suits my timetable."

"Where you headed?"

I never asked. I never thought I'd want to know. Kneeling, I pulled my luggage apart and ran my hand along the inner compartment. Maybe if I could get her to grab stuff from my bathroom...

"Texas. Austin."

A stupid ass grin spread over my face. "You don't say." I rolled my lips and made a decision. A shit one, but I had to play this out somehow. "Want a lift?"

"That's a long drive." She eyed me as I drew the drugs out of my pocket and lined the inner compartment with them. "I knew that's what you were doing," she said quietly.

"Yeah? Did it scare you?" My heart thumped traitorously in my chest.

"Nope."

"You say that a lot." I zipped the pouch and rocked back on my heels. "Want a ride in my noisy old truck instead of a communal public bus?"

She wrinkled her nose. "Hell, yes. You know, I thought you were from California."

"What makes you say that?" I kept my tone light though my shoulders tightened.

"Dunno." She shrugged and tossed her hair. "You seem like California. Sunshine and shit. I'll get my stuff. Don't you run off on me, baby oil boy," she warned.

A dopey ass grin left my cheeks aching, right up

until I had her strapped into my truck and turned over the engine that thankfully behaved itself. In fact, the grin lasted until we were several hours into the drive and she opened her laptop. Then a few things hit home real damn hard.

"Is this a fling where we go our separate ways at the other end?" I said quietly.

Skye swallowed. "Is this because I write articles you hate?" She peered at me through her lashes, and my dick swelled.

I shifted uncomfortably in my seat. "I don't wanna say goodbye to you, princess." My knuckles glowed white against the worn leather of my steering wheel.

"I don't want that either." She nibbled her lip.

I waited, but that seemed to be all she would say. My eyes squeezed tight, and I slapped my hand on the steering wheel. "Fuck it. Lying shits me and I made you a promise I don't want to break. I'm working with the Texas Ranger unit in Austin. I love what we have going, and screw it if that's the hopeless, soppy romantic in me coming out. But I don't want you thinking I'm some damn drug dealer. And...you're right. I was in California. As a firefighter in LA." I slammed my mouth shut, grinding my teeth. I didn't care if I just screwed myself seven ways to Sunday. She was worth it.

Skye mulled on that for a few miles. "So, you're a Texas Ranger, huh?" She twined her hands in her lap. "It was easier to believe you were a boy who loved fun and sun."

I raked my fingers through my hair. "I am. Usually. This was my first...job, or whatever. Kinda like an audition. If I fucked it up, then I don't get to stay, and I'll be going back to Cali. If I didn't screw it up, then I call Cali and I'm gonna make my boss real unhappy."

"You're good at your job?" She played with the hem of her pink cotton skirt with gold tassels.

"I have a lot of years in that job, and I know it well," I replied, trying to take my ego out of it.

"Sounds like you have a home there."

I breathed out. "Yeah, change is scary. But this offer came through and...I like the idea of being able to help. I don't know. That's stupid."

"It's not," she said in the same quiet tone I used with her before. A strange echo, but I got it. Kinda part of the snarky-fuck-frenzy-reflective vibe thing we had going on. "I think you'll suit it either way."

I slid my gaze across to her. "You know many Texas Rangers, Skye?"

She shrugged. "I've seen them getting medals, read about them in the paper. I live in Austin. It's impossible not to know about them."

"Fair enough." I swallowed and held out my arm.

She made a soft sound that kickstarted my heart, scooting across the bench and snuggling into my side. Her hand rested on my chest, her cheek on my shoulder. "You feel good."

"Yeah?" I kissed the top of her head. "So, we gonna try this thing when we get–" I cut that sentence off.

There was no guarantee I had the job. Hell, I already broke one of the cardinal rules, and we just left Mexico.

"I wanna try." She looked up at me and I swore I could fall into those blue eyes of hers and never come out. "No matter what happens. I can travel and stuff." She went back to studying her skirt.

My heart clenched. If I didn't get the job, I'd be back in LA and a firefighter didn't get the luxury or freedom of travel, or that many days off. Pulling overtime had been my life for the last few years, and I wasn't sure I could sit still for longer than a week on a beach.

"Whatever happens," I echoed, resting my cheek on her hair and tugging her closer. "Fuck it." I pulled over, throwing the truck into neutral and tipped her chin up.

"What–" Skye's protest died as I claimed her mouth, pushing her down onto the bench seat and kissed the hell out of both of us.

CHAPTER FIVE

HUDSON

I left Skye in my truck, unwilling to drop her off until I could tell her what sort of future I had. I couldn't think much beyond that while I stuffed the drugs into my jacket pockets, and kissed her thoroughly.

"You'll be great," she whispered, curling her fingers around my collar and pulling me down for one more kiss. "I have faith in you."

I was glad one of us did.

My jaw aching, I sucked in the vision of her perched on the bench seat, her tasseled gold and pink skirt fluttering around her stunning legs, a filmy floral blouse I nearly ripped open early in the trip in a need to be closer to her a soft contrast to her tan and the golden waves draped around her.

I walked into the Austin unit's headquarters in my jeans, boots and a t-shirt, not having shaved and looking exactly as I should for a twenty something hour drive with rest stops where I spent my time not looking at the road and my hand buried in Skye's pussy.

But now wasn't the time to think about that.

The office was empty except for Archer's closed door when I made it up the stairs, doing the deep breathing thing and probably sounding like a rampaging bull.

"Come in," Archer answered my knock.

I pushed the door open to the sparsest office I'd ever seen. My second time in it and the empty space still got me. A neat row of filing cabinets lined one wall, and a scarred wooden desk took up the space opposite the door, a single chair either side.

One was occupied by a man with red-brown longish hair, wearing a blue checked shirt, a worn leather ledger open on his desk that he closed as I entered.

"That looks like it gets about as much love as my steering wheel," I greeted him, pulling out the packets of drugs from my pockets and lining them up neatly by type on his desk, along with a list on my phone, including a description of everything I saw in Tijuana.

"Must love that truck then, Hudson. Good work," Archer said as I reached into my back pocket and pulled out the badge, placing it carefully before him and stepping back. "What's this?"

"It's yours." I kept my shoulders straight and stepped back.

I told Skye the truth. I wouldn't lie, not if I didn't have to.

"Is it?" Archer picked up the polished metal. "You know the history of these? They used to be made from Mexican pesos, a five and eight. Today, Rangers get two. One like this to carry day to day, and this sort." He pulled open a desk drawer and flicked a shiny metal badge my way.

I caught it one-handed and studied the coin set into a star. "It's solid history."

"It is." Archer shook his head when I extended my hand. "That's yours, Hudson."

I swallowed hard. "I broke your rules."

"Did you?" His gaze was unfathomable, but he made no move to take the badge from me. I placed it next to the other one on his desk and stepped back. "How?"

"I told a girl about the job. She came back with

me, and I hated lying to her, letting her think I ran drugs."

Archer nodded, his mouth opening. A rap from behind me nearly jerked me out of my skin. Archer didn't smile, though something flickered in his eyes.

"Come in."

The door opened and a tall woman in caramel pants and a white shirt entered the office. Her blonde hair was scraped back in a tight knot at the back of her neck. She held a white hat in her hands and stopped stiffly beside me.

If it wasn't for her blue eyes I might not have believed what I was seeing.

"Sir," Skye said in a hard voice.

I had nothing left. Everything we'd done...My stomach curled, and I breathed in hard. "Thank you for the experience, Archer. I'll leave you to it." I nodded respectfully, though Skye wouldn't even look at me, and made it as far as the door before Archer stopped me.

"Ranger." His voice sliced through the air, and even though I wasn't sure he was talking to me, I turned back. "Get your ass back here, Hudson. I'm not done."

"Sir." I reclaimed my spot on the worn carpet

beneath my feet, my movements as jerky as Skye's, who hadn't moved since she entered the room.

"Report." Archer watched me unblinkingly but spoke to Skye.

"The job was well executed. He might be a little unorthodox, but his methods worked well enough."

I tried not to grind my teeth and failed.

"Anything else?" Archer asked, leaning back in his chair.

"He broke cover on the way back." She didn't so much as look at me.

I swore my heart shattered right there and then.

"You weren't meant to travel together." Archer raised his eyebrows. "You changed the rules."

A tiny petal of hope painted in pinks and golds unfurled in my chest.

"Yes, sir." Skye stood rigid, her hands clasped behind her back, the knuckles white, the only outward expression of her tension. And like her face when I burst into her room in Tijuana, she was blank. Almost unreadable.

Except maybe to Archer. That man could be faced with a brick wall and deduce something from it. I'd put a full month's pay on that bet.

"Recommendation?"

She paused for a full minute while my heart

stalled with her. "He would be a solid asset if his morals don't trip him up."

Archer faced me in full, leaning forward. "Skye Hamilton was part of an older unit recently disbanded. She isn't used to how we run things here," –the corner of his mouth twitched, I swore– "but she's getting used to it. She also needs a partner." He collected both badges in his palm and held them out. "Job's yours, Hudson."

I swallowed. "I broke your rules." I seemed to be stuck on that.

"She changed them."

"We're good?"

"We are." Archer nodded, turning his attention to Skye. "Will working with Hudson be a problem?"

She breathed out hard through tight lips, her cheeks two spots of colour. "Not at all, sir."

"Good. He's your partner. There's a file on your desks. Dismissed." Archer opened his ledger and dropped his head.

And just like that I was a fully-fledged Texas Ranger.

I reached back, opening the door to his office. "After you," I murmured, the motion automatic.

The glare in her eyes wasn't.

Still frantic and untrusting.

Looked like I had a hell of a time before me to rebuild that with her. Because there was no chance I was letting her go.

"I knew those articles couldn't be real," I murmured as she passed me.

"They are fucking real, Hudson," she gritted out. "I've been writing them for years." Skye powered through the door, leaving me huffing a laugh in her wake.

"Hudson."

"Sir?" I pivoted sharply on my heel.

"Careful with her. She's had an abusive history. Not my story to tell."

Smiling faintly, I stepped into the doorway. "I know."

Archer nodded, the hint of a matching smile lighting his face as I pulled the office door shut.

I made it a good four steps to my desk, the one with my name on a damn engraved triangular thing, before Skye accosted me.

"You don't touch me, or kiss me, or–"

I ignored her outburst, and the new set of rules she tossed in my face and clasped her shoulders gently. "You got your say last time when you claimed me as your beach bodyguard. No, I don't care under what conditions." I pressed a finger over her lips.

"Here's my rules. Tell me everything. Don't hide shit from me. My side of that is I'll always have your back, no matter what. But I want to give this thing a go, Skye. I want to see if we can make it work."

"But what happened in Ti–"

"Was fucking amazing," I said softly, tucking a stray piece of gold hair behind her ear. "And for the record, this Skye is just as sexy as gold tasseled Skye and Bikini Skye."

"Objectifying," she muttered, her color heightening as she looked at me through her lashes.

"You bet your perfect fucking behind." I leaned in slowly, giving her time to pull away and kissed the corner of her mouth. "Gonna try this with me?"

She turned enough for me to capture her mouth in full. When I kissed her a little harder she didn't push me away, opening her lips and letting me in.

"Fine." She pulled back, and gave me sassy eyes. I couldn't wait to see what my handprint looked like on her ass. "Can we get to work now, Big Boy?"

"Keep it up, Skye. I'm keeping count." I slammed my hand down on my thigh, the crack reverberating around the room.

She held my gaze and raised her chin. "Do your worst, Hudson."

A grin spread over my face as I grabbed the file

and started flicking through, my mind already headed in other directions. "Oh, I plan to. Hell girl, I might even be able to show you what real love looks like."

Her eyes widened to the point of comical, and I pulled her to me for another heartfelt kiss, putting everything I was right behind that not-so-simple touch of lips on lips.

"You can't be serious," she whispered. "It's been a week."

I shrugged. *Fuck it*. What did I have to lose? Nothing but a stunning girl who happened to be my partner both day and night. "I'm all in, Skye. All for you."

"Romantic ass."

I huffed a laugh and tweaked her nose just to earn a glare.

Having Skye as both partner and girlfriend would be one hell of a challenge, but damn would I enjoy showing her all the ways a man could be romantic with a demanding woman he'd already fallen for, however long our partnership lasted.

Maybe for a long while.

Maybe forever.

There was no better way to test it than a road trip to South Carolina.

CHAPTER FIVE

SKYE

Hudson Whittingdon was a royal ass.

A sexy ass, an objectifying ass, and my brand spanking new partner.

Shit. Archer really pulled the wool over my eyes with that one and I was far from proud of it. Not that he seemed fazed that I slept with the newb, even though it horrified me more than a little bit. I assumed I'd be able to sweep the whole situation away as a summer fling in undercover work. That shit happened all the time. Then I'd transfer to another unit and the intimate skin-on-skin moments we shared would become stuff of urban legend.

Instead, my fling was my partner, confessing all

sorts of flowery bullshit I didn't believe in and now we were headed to...

Ba da ba boom—

A place called Love Beach. Hello, South Carolina. Where we were supposed to be newlyweds and keep an eye on a target that should never be part of our scope.

On the dash sat the plain gold band I was supposed to wear but couldn't bring myself to face the confining feeling, even if it was fake as fuck.

Hudson, the show off, put his on hours ago before we headed into Love Beach after our road trip.

No fucking lie. That's what the place was called, and we were headed there right now, with a fresh change of panties in a packed truck. The manilla folder sat in my lap and I once again sat gunshot in Hudson's truck heading into the stupidly-named town in South Carolina.

Instead of trying to even things with Hudson, or deal with the way he kissed me back in the office, I opted to ignore the huge beefy Ranger in the driver's seat and chose instead to study the small town's main street. Not overpopulated, it was still obvious which of those wandering along the row of shops and service providers was a local and which were the tourists purely by their dress.

The locals were much more laid back, and the travelers donned enormous floppy hats as their weapon of choice that had the locals dodging back on more than one occasion as they shared a sidewalk together.

The shops looked clean, if brightly colored, as if a family or PG rated movie vomited all over the place. And here we were, supposed to watch for a smuggler who escaped Texas Rangers on their own turf, study the target's habits, and bring back all our observations without doing a single thing to apprehend the man who took three lives on Texas land not a month before.

Was I impressed?

No ma'am, I was not.

Apparently, Archer hadn't got his ass in gear enough to get the man himself, but Hudson was as gung ho with this little test as he had been in Tijuana.

I wondered if his tastes in women and relationships fluctuated as fast as his attention. I rather suspected they did and I was simply a fast and furious summer passion in a long line of fling-like conquests reaching from California to Texas, no matter what he said back in the office, or any day since.

He kept insisting we were fine and it wasn't a week long thing.

Fine, two weeks, then.

The blur of color along the main street melded into a rainbow of pastels, and as soon as I noted the ice cream parlor on one end of a block, my stomach rumbled.

Hudson laughed, his deep voice reverberating around the cab in a far too appealing sound.

"Don't do that," I snapped.

"Do what?" He affected a wounded look, all puppy dog eyes, downturned mouth and wrinkly forehead.

I slapped the arm he slid across my shoulders, pushing him back. I sighed. The man was relentless, and not in a good way. Or maybe I did like his ways, and just hated that about myself, too.

I had a whole lot of hate for a stack of things right now.

I spotted something I didn't hate and threw out a hand, slapping the passenger window with my knuckles. "Stop here."

Hudson slammed on the brakes, eliciting a stream of honks behind us and dived into a space way too small for his monster of a vehicle. "This good?"

I pried open a squinted eye. "Do I need to order a funeral service for any small animals or grannies?"

"Hey, that's not nice. And you never know. Grannies in Texas be badass." He smirked.

I nodded at his nonsense and hauled my ass out of the truck. "Stay."

His laugh followed me as he bounded to the sideway and fell into step at my side. "Not a dog, Skye."

"But you're still my bitch." The barb was hollow and meaningless. A wave of tiredness hit me. "Where are we staying?"

"I mean, I'm happy to be your bitch but my girl's gotta tell me what's up, otherwise I can't take care of her. 'Kay?" He nuzzled my temple.

I batted him away before I could catch something, like feelings.

Already did that.

I ignored my annoying voices, too.

"We're working. We don't have time for things like this." I lifted my pace.

Hudson matched me step for step. "You're hell bent on this investigation, huh?" The back of his hand brushed mine and I repressed the shiver that raced through my body and along my arms, turning into Caffeine Beach, the coffee shop I spotted earlier.

"I'm hell bent on getting this done, going home and starting real work," I snapped back. "Not going to apologize, because this is a bullshit assignment, much like the last."

"Aw, Archer wouldn't do that to us. He needs this information." Hudson caught my hand this time, linking our fingers together. His were thicker and speared my fingers apart. I hated that I liked the feeling that he was bigger than me. Could actually take everything I threw at him.

Not appropriate on the job.

Besides, I knew a few things about his precious Archer that he clearly didn't.

Like that the man wasn't invested in the unit and was closing up shop, handing the unit over to the next most capable man, and heading north. Real far north, like Montana. Borderlands area. About as far as a person could get without actually needing a passport.

But I didn't say any of that because a large part of me knew I would need it for a rainy day sometime. Maybe soon.

I yanked my hand free. "You don't call having no arrest at the end of the assignment progress?" I walked straight up to the counter. "Giant long black please, four shots, no sugar. Thanks." The waitress looked at me doubtfully, but wrote down my order without any more questions, thankfully.

"Well we are on this one, so why don't you start behaving less like a cop and more like the girl I'm supposed to have just married?" Hudson whispered in my ear, flicking his tongue along the curve in a way that liquefied and overheated all of my internal functions.

I shivered lightly against him, and made to push him back but the smart ass expected the move and caught my wrists, twirling me expertly in his arms. The moment my mouth opened to protest, he covered it with his in a seriously pornographic kiss that would have ended in bed had we been in an enclosed space. Instead, my red face flamed along with probably anyone else in the shop who couldn't possibly avoid the PDA he put on.

"Aren't you overdoing it?" I whispered, looking coyly up at him through my lashes, fluttering them and stepping on his toes to let him know he crossed a line.

The big boof didn't buy into my play. His expression grew serious, and it stalled me, the way he looked at me, all intense and complicated.

Life needs to be simple. In and out. Hi and bye.

I couldn't do complicated any more, not now or ever. Never again.

I couldn't.

The corners of Hudson's lips turned up in the sort of sexy smile that left me leaning into him whether my brain screamed at me to retain my independence, or not.

"Aw, come on, Skye. I just found you. Don't ruin my day." His fingers knotted around my hand as his mouth lowered over mine, leaving just enough space for a single breath before he kissed me again.

A dare to defy him in public.

Spoilers: I didn't.

His tongue dragged over mine, his pace slow, but dominating, a reminder of the way he fucked me by the beach in Mexico. A moan caught in my throat before I remembered where we were.

When he pulled back, he wore a satisfied smirk and a gold band sat on my left ring finger.

Asshole.

CHAPTER SIX

HUDSON

Skye bamboozled me at every turn. Back on the beach she could have been an ice queen, for fuck's sake. In Texas, I got to see the hard ass side that appealed to Archer enough that he hired her.

Here in South Carolina? She ran hot as Hades, but sure as hell it wasn't at me.

Because that ring on her finger scared the daylights outta her, and everyone around us could see her fear right there on display.

My stomach cramped. I slung an arm around her, pulling her into my chest. "Easy, honey," I murmured.

Fuck, this assignment will be blown before we

touch foot in our apartment. A joint holiday—ahem, honeymoon—apartment with one bed, ostensibly.

Guess I'm sleeping on the sofa.

"Don't *honey* me," she snapped, but thankfully my shirt muffled the sound and only I heard it. Maybe.

An older couple eyed us, and I gave them what I hoped was a Californian winning grin. What a way to do fifty states in five minutes. The girl sent my head on a whirlwind tour of my own sanity. How the hell we were supposed to be partners in this thing while all I wanted to do was find a quiet space and fuck like bunnies for the next hour eluded me.

Her, too, from the dazed look in her eyes.

Huh. I liked that one.

"Don't do that," she murmured, a little softer, thankfully.

"All part of the show." I affected a swagger I sure as hell didn't feel with her looking at me with a decent dollop of distrust as she swiped her fingers— glittering with that ring—over her pink mouth I just wanted to kiss some more.

Because she tasted like sunshine and sand and new beginnings and I never wanted to stop.

"We have a job to do," she reminded me, one

hand still curled in my shirt from our PDA. She looked down at it, surprise written across her stunning features, and pried her fingers free, flexing them.

"Way to give a guy a boner and whiplash in one. This is the assignment, *honey*," I said pointedly.

"What, being a demanding asshole?" She pivoted in the circle of my arms, and stared around. "Ah, there's a good place to start." She strode forward, or tried to, but I pulled her back.

"Teamwork. There's no I in it, Skye."

"Exactly. So we do this my way."

"Or we find our accommodation and get it done the Archer way."

Her laugh tinkled around me like silver bells before her voice sliced through the effect laced heavily with derision. "There's brown on your nose, Ranger. Did you know?" Her hair flicked me in the face as she marched forward.

I caught her hand, catching up with her all too easily, and fast enough I noted the tight expression on her face before she managed to hide it.

Ahh. That explained a lot. Perhaps our cover story was a little too good.

"You can be the Ranger if you want," I said

softly. "I'll be satisfied with being the house husband."

Her brow dipped though she didn't look at me. "I don't think anyone would buy that."

"And yet here you are." I squeezed her hand. "Busting past all the odds and expectations of failure."

She stopped short. "What did you say?"

I caught her chin. "What aren't you saying, princess?" She said nothing and I smiled slightly. "Hit a nerve, huh?"

Her gaze drifted past me and before I could snark at her further, her expression cleared and she pulled her hand from mine.

"Stay here, househusband."

"Is this how it's always going to be?" I called to her sexy backside that disappeared inside a jewelry shop.

"Better catch her now. Not a good habit to get into already." The older gent and his wife winked at me.

I managed a smile and followed Skye toward the shop she disappeared into, nearly face planting right into her as she busted back on out.

"Whoa. That was fast. Didn't find what you wanted?" I asked carefully.

Skye beamed at me. "Nope. Got exactly what I wanted."

I waited for more but there was nothing forthcoming.

"Hope it was his credit card, love." The matching lady with the older gent called gaily, waving a bag that looked cute and colorful, and probably cost a month's wage.

Skye laughed, nope. Not laughed. Giggled. My girl *giggled*. The sound stunned me for a moment before I pulled my shit together and slipped my arms around her waist.

She didn't so much as flinch, leaning into me and rising up onto her toes right there in the doorway to the jewelry shop.

"I found our mark-co," she sang softly, shuffling her feet to let the next customer out.

The guy stood at least as tall as me and looked like something from the Godfather—or maybe the rap sheet in the manilla folder that Skye cuddled the entire way to South Carolina.

Tall, dark and broody looking, the dude looked like he could scent a bad deal or a weak chin a mile away. Or maybe a fake pair of tits.

Because right now my mark had eyes for one person.

Skye.

His gaze dropped down her body like he planned on undressing her. She giggled again, shimmying against me and more than one thing rose to attention.

Fortunately, it was my temper that cooled first as I hauled her against me and out of his way.

"This way, Skye. Let the gentleman pass," I forced out pleasantly through gritted teeth.

"Not a problem at all." He placed a hand on Skye's shoulder and trailed his finger along her arm. "Is it, darlin'?"

She fucking well *sighed* into me.

The hell?

"Not at all, Marco. This is my husband, Hudson. Say hi to the nice man, Huddy," she giggled again.

That noise was starting to get to me.

"Hi," I said politely when my brain froze on the image of spanking the sound right out of her. From the look on Marco's face, I wasn't alone in my assessment of her behavior. "Do you to know each other?"

"Oh no," Said Skye, her face pink with the half-truth.

"Yes," said Marco, looking me straight in the eye and offering a smirk. "Marcus Torrino. Or Marco." He shrugged.

Got yourself a gangland name there, Mister Marco Torrino?

Either name would flag with Interpol and a dozen smaller home-based units, including ours. Archer took me through the process, and Brodie after on a fast call to bring me up to date. What I couldn't work out was how Miss Skye made a new friend in thirty seconds or less in a shop.

"Oh, Marco reads my blog." Skye looked up at me, her eyes shining, and blushed.

"Ah." My brain blanked totally. No wonder she looked so damn happy, especially after I tore her apart for her opinions. "And, uh, what do you think?"

God, I hoped my profile said I was meant to be stupid, because I fucking well sounded like it.

"Yes, he loved the one about empowering women. You remember the one you read on the beach?" Her smile remained, though her eyes turned hard.

"Yes." I broke her gaze and grinned at Marco. "She loves pulling a guy apart."

"Indeed." His eyes never left her. "I have a party on my yacht tonight. At Passion Cove. The *Serenade*. Would you like to attend?" His gaze lifted and his smirk that she seemed to eat right up remained.

"Both of you, of course. I'm sure I can find something for you to do while I entertain your...wife."

Fuck me if the leech wasn't hitting on her right in front of me and telling me he'd fuck her while I drank his boat dry.

It's an assignment.

She's a summer fling.

And summer felt like it was already nearly over. Maybe a little too fast for my liking.

The truth was that I didn't want this thing with her to end, though it likely had to if we were to remain partners and not end up hating each other. I foresaw a whole lot of nights alone in my new place in Texas with my hand as company while she partied hard on yachts with this crook.

Cover job or not, I wasn't ready to let her sell herself just for a case that, like she said, was going nowhere. But it might in future. I knew the Ranger unit worked to feed information to various police precincts on different cases and helped out as an umbrella to pass down information.

On the other hand I understood the need to close up a test case like this as fast as possible and earn a few hat feathers like Skye wanted.

It just wasn't going to be on this job. And I didn't

have to like another man touching her, cover story be damned.

"I'm sure we can make time. After we find our accommodation and...break it in," I said baldly, squeezing Skye until she squeaked and shot me a sexy as hell death stare.

"Definitely." She ignored me pointedly when I kissed along her shoulder, overplaying the enamored honeymooner. She dug her blunt nails into the back of my hands until I was certain they would bear little crescent moons in perpetuity. "What time tonight, Marco?"

The smile she gave him was nothing like the tight ones she offered me the entire trip.

"Shall we say nine o'clock? Or a little later. I don't mind waiting."

I'm sure you don't, asshole.

"We'll make good use of the time," I promised her, mentally adding a pink peachy ass into that equation.

"We'll see you then," Skye promised.

"Make sure you wear something...nice." He smiled at her, and it turned slimier if such a thing was possible as he glanced at me, amusement lighting his eyes. "Something suitable."

"Can do," I said softly, meeting his gaze and

letting a little of my own fire through the mask I donned the moment we stepped out into the main street of Love Beach.

You wanna play hard, motherfucker? I'll play hard.

"I can't wait," Skye oozed, letting me tow her away before I blew something, like my temper.

Or the case, before it started.

CHAPTER SEVEN

SKYE

I slithered into the dark blue dress after my shower in the main bathroom while Hudson muttered away darkly to himself in the ensuite. The room at Garden House—the entire hotel—was amazing. Everything was color coded. Everything was neat, tidy and looked brand spanking new. The honeymoon suite was more like a presidential suite and I didn't want to know how much the unit shelled out for this little project. Mind, I also didn't know the budget and expectations Archer set, and any new piece of tech could cost more than a week's stay in a place like this.

The bedroom was filled with lace and gold and pinks, with a real fake pink bear rug on the floor, like some sixties or seventies flick regurgitated brand new décor. The effect was fun and flirty, and the amount of details did my head in.

Not that Hudson said much as he towed me inside the room, making sure to kiss me thoroughly on the threshold before pushing me inside with a hard hand that promised naughty things later on.

Naughty things I might or might not crave even if indulging him was a really bad idea.

It seemed smart to get out of his reach until he cooled a little after our chance encounter with our target for the week. Not that I thought getting the required information would take half as much time as Archer expected. My hand brushed the screen of my phone while I contemplated asking for extra duties.

Marco might be a leech, but he was a simple one though dirty in more than the sexual sense, though I knew that was true of him also. Closing up our assignment part B meant heading back to Texas post haste, and maybe going our separate ways. I agreed to partnering with Hudson to get into the unit. Surely it wouldn't be that hard to also extract myself from him.

Hudson showed himself to be possessive, which

meant little freedom, more judginess from Mister McSook, not only too passionate in his...work, but also impractical. Partnering with a constantly green eyed monster was along the lines of my worst nightmare. At the least it meant constantly dealing with possessiveness and the lack of independence which I fought so freaking hard for.

Shaking my hair out, I curled it and left it hanging half down my back, fixing sapphire and diamond earrings to my ears. The dress, one from a different life that Archer suggested might be the sort of attire I'd need on this assignment as though he knew and was still testing us like an overbearing father figure, fit as well as it did the last time I wore it.

I just hoped tonight worked out a whole lot better than last time.

"Skye? I hope you're ready. We need to be there in a bit if we want to scope the place out before we— holy shit." Hudson, as eloquent as ever, halted in the doorway to the main bathroom, his bowtie hanging around his neck and fingers grasping either side like he wasn't sure what to do with it.

I finished with my lipstick and straightened, running my hands along my sides, knowing he'd like it. What? A girl has to get her rocks off somehow and it wouldn't be either of the men who wanted in—or out—of the dress tonight who made me smile next.

"Glad you scrub up well," I murmured, smiling slightly and trying not to drool.

It wasn't only the bowtie that was still undone—I was back to beach bodyguard Hudson, all tan, muscles and tequila nights. So far I'd only seen him in board shorts, or jeans and a tee. Anything else seemed out of uniform for the bulky man. But it wasn't a lie – he did scrub up good. Black pants showed off hard earned thigh muscle, and an expanse of golden skin above the belt line, which was where I fixed my gaze.

On the skin. Above the belt.

Shit, shit, shit.

I glanced up and by the smirk that decorated his drooly face as he surveyed me in kind I knew I'd been busted. His hair was pushed back off his face like a blonde James Bond, all suave and shit.

"Where'd my partner go?" I said without thinking,

"Yeah." He swallowed, his eyes still fixed on me. "Same, honey."

I shook my head, though I wasn't sure if it was at him or me. "If you want the tie done up, then you need to do the shirt up." I clicked my tongue and batted his hands away when he obediently started to button from the bottom up. "No. Never bottom. Start at the top."

"What are you, a reclusive socialite turned Texas Ranger?" he gaped at me as I deftly did his shirt up, avoiding his skin as best I could and made a not so mess of his bow tie.

"There."

"You are a goddess, you know that?" One hand rose to brush over a curl I painstakingly twisted and sprayed until it stayed that way. "And I get to have you."

"Not tonight, sunshine." I batted that hand away too and stepped back, the spell holding us in a sort of charged stasis breaking.

"You wound me," he said softly, not stepping away like I expected, or huffing at me. "He's gonna be trouble tonight. You know that."

I swallowed back the urge to snap but the wounded look on Hudson's face shattered something fragile inside me. Guilt swamped me and I softened my tone. "He's not the only one who'll be trouble." I stepped into him a little. "It's a job, Hudson. Let this thing go."

His brow furrowed. "Why? Because we're partners? If it's because you don't trust me, then seek another Ranger to fuck and dump." The line of his jaw remained hard. He stared at me, his anger turning inward as his body stiffened.

"Maybe it's best." I let out a breath. *That was easier than I expected.*

Then why did I feel so damn shitty about it?

"It's time." Hudson checked his watch, offering no reprieve. "If you get stuck tonight I'll be there, Skye." His voice lowered. "I promise."

I shook my head and gave him an empty smile. "You can't promise me anything at all."

Yep, tonight was going to be just like last time.

I padded across the floor to the door and slipped on my heels that almost brought me to Hudson's height, but not quite. Marco didn't like tall women, and I wondered if I should dumb it down a little more. He seemed to like the bimbo act after all.

"Beautiful," Hudson murmured, right at my elbow. His fingers curled through my arm. "Let's get this show on the road so we can pack the hell up and go home."

We'd only been in the town for a handful of hours and I was more than ready to agree.

If only on that one thing.

* * *

The *Serenade* sat moored beside other multimillion dollar yachts on the waterfront. Marco's personal party wasn't the only one in progress. Further along the bay, another boat thumped with music and laughter that carried across the water. Marco's was a small gathering in comparison, but the guest list was that much more exclusive. Without my accidental meeting with the smuggler—whose boat was easily the largest and most expensive in the bay, though I doubted he needed the tax write-off like the software developer's boat we passed earlier, we would never have been able to get on board.

Thank Archer for suggesting we both pack cocktail and black tie attire. It was like he'd known how this assignment would go. Setting aside my instinctive dislike for the man abandoning his unit for a moment, I wondered what else he might expect, and if we would live up to the pedestal he set out for us.

"Behave tonight, and I promise I'll make it worth your while later," Hudson murmured in my ear. His hand slunk around my waist, pulling me back into him. "And I'll let you choose the activity."

"What if I don't pick your favorite thing?" I

asked absently, falling back into our usual, snarky banter.

"But you're my favorite thing." He licked the shell of my ear. "If you fuck him, I'll turn this ass red with one hand and then start with the other."

A shiver rippled over me at the thought, both terrifyingly satisfying and abhorrent in equal measure. "You and your dirty promises."

"Will you take me up on one?" His fingers drifted lower, grazing the front of my dress that didn't feel half the shield that it had been when I first dressed in it. The walk into the cove was wonderful in the way that it cleared my head, but walking next to Hudson when he was brooding.... hurt. In all sorts of ways.

He's not for me.

And yet...he was. Hudson was nothing like the sort of man I usually dated, and I hadn't gone on a date for a long time. Not to say I didn't have one night stands and too many that I was able to forget the first shoddy attempts that got worse by the pick-up. But he offered something I hadn't had—ever.

Security.

I should jump at the opportunity to have someone dote on me but that sort of closeness, the intimacy he needed—that was the terrifying part.

Not his hand on my ass, or me sleeping with someone else. It was the thought that the security he offered might be there one day, and...gone the next.

Cliché, but true.

I'd been there, had it happen, and had to walk away for my own sanity. I sure as hell couldn't do it again.

That was my game. Cement the future of my career. Little to no risk in my personal life, no matter what it took.

But to do that I'd have to break a Ranger's heart.

"Skye, we should have talked—" Hudson started,

"My newest toy." Marco's voice echoed around the boat and the water, gesturing us onto the one hundred million dollar yacht that by rights belonged to someone else, and registered under another man's name, or perhaps another name of Marco's. He had a few, like a collection.

His hands swept out as he said those words, but his gaze remained firmly on me.

Hudson's touch fell away from me, and cold air brushed my back where he stood a moment before, leaving me alone with Marco.

"Don't worry. He's already off doing something he'll find...fun." The corner of Marco's mouth turned up in a dark promise that either meant he expected my new husband to earn himself a night's worth of lap dances from an expensive hooker, or flat his way across the bay come dawn.

It was going to be one of those nights, and I understood this game well.

From the look in Marco's eyes, he expected at least a little better behavior from me than Hudson, and I was more than willing to oblige. For now.

"I'm all yours." I took the hand he extended, my fingers brushing the dark purple silk weave he wore than on a white man might have looked ostentatious but with Marco's Spanish heritage, actually looked quite classy. The open, crisp white shirt beneath spoke of an extra sort of expectation.

"Oh, I know." He leaned down to brush his lips across my ear, erasing Hudson's touch I hated at the time and missed now.

I steeled myself, tipping my chin up and smiling as vapidly as I could. "What game are we playing tonight?" I'd bet my new salary that Marco had something in mind. He always did.

"My favorite game, Miss Skye." He held out his other hand, gesturing me downstairs.

The door shut and the lock flicked before I really heard his words...and the fact I didn't pick him up on it.

Pivoting slowly on my heel I turned to correct his mistake and found myself forehead to barrel with a matte black gun, close enough to read the serial number—if the damn thing hadn't already been filled off.

Double shit.

CHAPTER EIGHT

HUDSON

I didn't make it three steps across the back of the *Serenade* before I knew something was badly wrong.

Sure, Marco was hosting a party—a closed one, with cartel heads openly on the water in front of me. These were men I knew from the flick through of potential guests in Archer's folder that were hot prospects. The hottest sort that rarely showed their faces to an area with CCTV, and certainly not together.

And every single one of them were banded together on the back of the yacht, drinking and making fucking merry.

The only one missing was Marco.

"Cognac, sir?" a server offered politely.

"Thank you." I swallowed my misgivings and selected a cup from the tray he held, inhaling the scent appreciatively, wishing I had Skye by my side to slap some sense into me.

He nodded and moved on, leaning in to speak quietly with the next tuxedoed attendant.

Damnit, everywhere I looked I saw a threat. To her, to everyone in the bay.

We just got here and the whole place looked ready to go right to hell in a heartbeat. I didn't have my girl by my side, no matter how much she fought against the need that linked us both.

Over a week on the beach in Tijuana, a road trip and now this operation...she hadn't slapped me yet, though I was fairly sure she would have if she didn't expect to get herself fired for the effort.

Something told me that Archer wasn't that sort of boss, unless the occasion truly called for it, and it was one of the reasons I crossed state lines to meet him in Texas. Skye's reasons for not trusting him... they were her own, along with the hang ups she had about relationships.

If we survived tonight, that girl and I were sitting in the pinked out room that looked like a certain panther got toey with a paint brush, and hashing it out.

Right before I fucked her to sleep, and not in the boring way.

As if the girl wasn't complicated enough without tonight's clusterfuck in the making ready to burst from the wings.

"-ing, sir?" One of the cartel heads—I couldn't recall a name on the spot—brought me out of my day dreams and left me floundering on the back deck of a multi-million dollar yacht.

"I'm sorry. Honeymoon and all. My head is still..." I shrugged and let a goofy smile slide across my face as I caught the eye of a stocky Mexican looking man and nearly fell flat on my ass.

The one ace I had up my sleeve should I need it.

Brodie Martinez.

I wondered if Archer gave Skye the same undercover talk I got, or if Brodie was here to babysit the newb? Right now I didn't care. I was in over my head and would take all the help I could get.

"He's got his head up something, that's for sure." The stocky long term undercover Ranger with ties to cartels going back a long way elbowed my ribs and gave me a slightly leering grin. His stare hardened, daring me not to play along.

I put on the only persona I was able to come up with at short notice: the dumb ass goofball of a man with more money than sense.

As long as Skye stayed out of trouble, I'd be able to hold onto it.

"That's what new wives are for, before they become old wives," someone said to a round of jeering laughter. "Salute." The man raised his glass, clinking mine and everyone else's as they drank their varied spirits I could barely identify, being a JD and coke boy from way back.

Brodie laughed along with them, his foot hitting the back of my calf until I joined the hilarity that went on and on. Then I made the mistake even I knew not to make. I downed my cognac in one.

It took me less than a minute for the boat to sway beneath my feet, and then I couldn't feel the rest of me at all.

I woke with numb hands linked tightly behind my back. The silver bracelets bit into my skin, but the only thing I saw before me were a pair of tits I didn't recognize right in my face.

No one likes a dirty cadaver in any case. I ignored

the warning voices in my head and looked around at the roof that told me I was somewhere inside the yacht, from the sway of the boat, rather than a luxury warehouse on the dock.

At least there's still a good chance my body would be dumped in the water.

The stripper attached to the tits in my face ground away on my lap to no avail as I stared blankly up at her.

"Come on, baby. We can have fun." She cooed, sexy like. Or maybe it was supposed to be sexy, but the girl could do with a mint yesterday and every day for the rest of my life.

"Get off me," I said softly, trying to keep a rein on my politeness.

"Can't hold his liquor, eh?" One of the men from the deck called.

I shook my head and managed to slide on my stupid ass grin that was starting to hurt, doing a head-count that told me I was outnumbered five to one. Four, if I counted Brodie.

I've attended fires that smelled better than this place.

"Come on, baby." The girl rubbed her dry crotch over my equally unresponsive lap. "You can get it up."

"Afraid not. Always was a cheap drunk." I smiled at her, letting my eyes empty of emotion. Everyone else saw a stupid honeymoon lovelorn; she saw a man who pulled bodies from fires that no longer looked human and lived the last few years having nightmares about them because I wasn't about to fess up and go to counseling, just to torture myself further.

She got a glimpse of *that* man, and she moved her string bikini clad tush fast enough that I could breathe again after a few seconds and not inhale her stale-sex scent.

Marco might like another man's slops or think himself a cuck-king, but there was no chance in hell I was putting my cock in a stripper when Skye was all that consumed me since she announced me as her bodyguard for the summer.

Since the day she first flounced down on the beach beside me.

Fucking fail there.

Hell, I hoped she was alright.

I shook my head, playing it up to the crowd of drinking men, wondering what the hell Marco's game was. "Come on, guys. I already had my bachelor's party. The stripper there could shoot things out of her pussy and hit a target."

Fortunately the stripper they set on me scampered and wasn't there to claim I was talking shit out of my ass at this point.

Stay with the character. It builds doubt.

And doubt breeds, face to face.

Those were Brodie's last words to me on the brief call we had before I took off with Skye to our new beach destination. He never told me he'd be here. Though I was grateful, I wasn't really ready for more surprises.

This was meant to be a surveillance mission, after all.

"I thought we might pay a little game of truth or dare." Marco appeared through a door at the back of the room, beyond the crowd of men who parted to let him pass. "You see, I ask you a question, and you dare me not to pull the trigger for the answer."

I kept my inane smile plastered across my face. "I don't remember this game being played quite that way. But then, maybe California's a different beast." I shrugged.

Marco didn't smile back. "I think you mean Texas, Mister Ranger. Isn't that right, Skye? Isn't this the man you had to trap in order to bring him right here, to me?"

Skye slipped out from behind Marco, her face

closed, though still stunning. "That's right," she said, robotically.

Girl needs acting lessons. Or maybe it wasn't as obvious to everyone else in the room. Her false front sure as shit was to me.

"Whatcha doing, honey?" I said, mustering a little fake cheer, and letting it drop inch by inch, as though the reality was setting in. A double whammy, really, as this situation was all sorts of FUBAR. My heart wanted to pound, but too many years of fire-fighting prevented me from losing my shit just yet.

Thank Christ, as the way she looked at me then at Marco left my blood running colder than a chilled beer in winter.

"My job, dear," she said sugary sweetly, glaring at me.

CHAPTER NINE

SKYE

Lying to Hudson wasn't quite like lying to anyone else. He didn't look all butt hurt, nor did he get that fake–I only suspected it was a fake–expression that told me I wounded him somewhere deeper inside.

No, Hudson looked at me with anger underlying that stupid ass expression he plastered over his face and refused to drop.

He better not drop it. We'd both be dead if Marco had any inkling on how badly I lied to him.

And Hudson's anger would be that much easier to weather than my ex's.

Marco's arm slithered around my waist, pulling me into him like it was a place where I'd always fit.

But that wasn't quite the reality. I used to fit against him, once. I used to trust him. And becoming a Ranger when Archer knew my history was the toughest damn thing I'd ever had to do.

Then he sent us on this godforsaken mission and I knew–*I knew*– the man hated me with everything in him.

Because he just signed my death warrant sending me right back in, and probably Hudson's, too,. That was the part that hurt, the trust we built inadvertently, despite me pushing him away as much as possible.

Okay, so I did a seriously shitty job of pushing him away because being in Hudson's arms was *nice*. And no one talks about how good *nice* is until it's ripped away. All the things you don't see and appreciate when you should, and all.

Every one of my lies to him, to his face, by omission-–they all danced between us while Marco breathed down my collar like he wanted to rip of my clothes and fuck me right in front of Hudson just to prove a point.

Knowing Marco, he probably would.

I saw the moment the penny dropped for Hudson. It wasn't pretty and I swore I heard the big man's heart break from across the room, right as

Marco's hand plunged into the neckline of the dress I should never have worn and mauled my breast without permission.

"I remember buying this dress for you," he murmured into my ear, squishing my flesh like a stress toy.

I closed my eyes and pretended to be somewhere else. A beach on Tijuana, maybe. Back in bed with Hudson. On cue my nipple hardened and Marco let out a truly horrendous groan that flushed me with embarrassment and doused my arousal all over.

"Don't touch me." I jerked away from him, fixing my dress and cast my gaze anywhere except at Hudson.

I'm sorry. I should have said something.

I should have said a lot of things.

Archer gave us a hellbent, two day shunt across the country to knock out the bugs. I used my time poorly, ignoring Hudson, cradling my hurt and fear to my chest in the most unhealthy way possible.

And look where that landed us.

Not just me, but him, too.

"I'm sorry," I muttered, still daydreaming about the cottage behind the beach.

"Don't worry, sweetheart, you will be," Marco snarled, fisting my hair and wrenching me back. "Or didn't you want to give your new boyfriend the show we planned?"

I winced, breathing hard through my nose to control myself. "There is no fucking *we*, Marco, and there hasn't been for a very long time."

He growled, snatching my hand in front of his face. "My ring used to be here. *Mine*, Skye. You understand no piece of paper can take that right from me."

I glared at my ex, my mouth set in a hard line and watched the intent to murder enter Marco's eyes. This was it, then. The reason I left him before I understood how dirty the man was and not in all the right ways. Why I walked away when he was across the country, trafficking women and drugs I didn't know about at the time and requested regularly to help put to bed once I became a Ranger.

I was told I was too close to be put on the case, and his name slipped to the bottom of the pile. One man gave me the chance, knowing I didn't want to work for him, and look how well my *wish granted* moment was turning out.

Just like history repeating itself, Marco raised a hand and slashed it across my face.

The move was so familiar I didn't flinch, didn't even feel the burn as my head snapped back until my neck kinked with the sharp action. Then the pain set in, and with it came the all too once commonplace fear that froze me in place.

"Aw, crying already?" Marco mocked me as he swiped his fingers across my numb cheeks.

"Am I?" I blinked at him, not even trying to pull away. Nausea rose up my stomach, and I fought the bile back the moment it bit my tongue. That I did have control over, if nothing else. If Marco was going to kill me tonight, I didn't want to puke on his shoes and give him the satisfaction of staining my dignity along with ending my life.

"I told you, *mine,*" he gloated, lording over me.

All just the usual day for me. Three years of relative freedom disappeared with a blink, but not before Hudson turned the tables and put his life before mine.

"But she's not yours," he said, that goofy smile still curling into his voice though I wasn't looking at him. "She's mine. Ring on her hand says so."

I closed my eyes. *You stupid fucking, brave, wonderfully goofy man.* Marco would have killed him before but now he'd take Hudson's tongue, his fingers, and probably some other part of his anatomy and feed it to him before he bled out on the yacht's deck.

"A fake ring." Marco raised his chin, glaring down his nose at the man handcuffed across the room.

A tiny twitch in Hudson's shoulders drew my attention to the man who *had* been handcuffed a moment ago.

Boy's got skills.

Maybe we weren't dead yet.

CHAPTER TEN

HUDSON

I gave Skye the same dopey grin I gave Marco, like I didn't believe the situation for a minute, but this time my gaze held a message in it.

It seemed my ace in the hole turned up on time... just as planned.

Because like Skye, Archer gave me a different mission. I just hadn't realized how in depth hers was...or how personal.

Skye stalled, her breath shortening as she watched me, and swept a hand across her back and came up empty. That didn't come as a surprise; I didn't expect her to be packing in the dress she wore.

The way the asshole had his hands on her, however...that did need addressing.

The ring on her finger might be fake but the intention wasn't. She mine to love, and I'd protect her like she was, even if she decided otherwise the minute we were out of here and the man all too familiar with her sexy as fuck body. I Kept that stupid ass expression on as I loosened the handcuffs around my wrists. A pro of having a boss who was an ex-cop for many decades before he switched services. That man taught us all sorts of little tricks, and right now I was damn glad of that one.

My helping hand shifted behind Marco. Thanks to Skye's breasts suddenly pressed to his chest and the paw she allowed to grope her ass, he didn't notice the speed a big man can move at, or the gun pressed to the back of his head. Brodie nodded to me and disappeared back into the shadows. It seemed that was the man's natural habitat.

Right now, this was my rodeo. If I fucked up, he was there to clean up the mess–not save my ass.

"Let the pretty girl go, and we only have a small problem." I dangled the handcuffs in front of Marco's face.

Skye huffed a laugh. "Give me those." She jumped for them and Marco spun, his hand on her waist and his other in his pocket.

I didn't think twice. I fired.

He stood before me, a blank look on his face before his body crumpled, a hole decorating his temple.

"Born and bred in Texas," I said softly.

My gaze caught and held Skye's as someone cheered behind us. I didn't hear anything else while Brodie worked crowd control. I had no idea if I was headed for jail but the concept of not seeing Skye again hurt more than anything else.

Ignoring any threat around us, I reached for her and for once, she came to me without a fight, letting me claim her mouth in a kiss bred by pure desperation on a party night at Love Beach.

Three hours later and with a lot of repetition on our respective stories, Skye and I were back in our pink as fuck apartment at Garden House. Brodie pulled rank, which sat well with the FBI agent who also lurked on the yacht, and things moved quickly after that.

Apparently Archer had a deal with an undercover cop and slipped us into an ongoing investigation on Marco Torrino...with slightly unexpected results. No one planned for more than an arrest to take place, but Skye became the wild card Marco apparently obsessed about for years once they split. And now I was left with a shaking girl who refused to talk or do anything else than let me hold and kiss her.

Hey, it was a start. I'd take that, considering I just killed the last man she was with on any permanent basis, from what she said to the local cops But she didn't say anything else to me. At least, not yet.

Skye shifted in my arms, burrowing closer. "Winungging?" she asked into my shirt.

I'd go with it, needing the skin to skin contact, but I didn't think she'd appreciate that after the way her ex mauled at her.

"Say that again?" I asked softly, stroking her hair.

"I said," –she came up for air– "why aren't you running all the way back to Texas without me?"

I frowned, still playing with her hair. Soft curls twirled around my finger and I gave an experiment tug, drawing her closer. "Why would I run?"

"Because I'm toxic to everything I touch." She frowned back at me. "You saw me with Marco. I haven't apologized. But you saved my life and I'm..."

"In shock," I supplied, keeping my voice low and

tucking her body into mine. "Right now, all I want is my girl safe. If that means not talking, then I'll wait until you want to." *If* she wanted to talk. There was no guarantee and no way I'd push her before she was ready.

Archer gave me that tip back in his office, and it was a damn fine one.

"Why are you so *nice*," she asked desperately, reaching up to trace her fingers along my jaw.

The light caress was the sweetest thing I'd ever experienced. It didn't take long before she arched up, offering me her mouth as consolation for the words that weren't coming out. I took that second prize and ran with it.

Pink bear rug be damned, I rolled her onto her back, stretching my body along hers and kissed her until she softened beneath me. My mind was full of conflict, the need to say something–anything–about what happened on the boat killing me but the moment I opened my mouth she shut it for me.

"Not now. Not yet," she whispered. "Just... forgot. Everything."

"Not you," I whispered, cupping her jaw and sliding my tongue into her mouth.

Her legs curled around my hips, her heels urging me to rub against her, but that need from before to have skin on skin contact drew me back. I shucked my shirt onto the floor, trailing my fingers along the terry toweling robe she threw on seconds after entering the apartment, barely letting go of my hand to rip her dress off and throwing it into a corner of the room.

"I want you closer," I murmured, staring down at her.

My girl was hurting and I'd give her anything she wanted, but right now I also needed to know I wasn't pushing her past limits she'd regret in the morning.

Like fucking the man who killed her ex. Her smarmy ex, a crook, and all the things that went along with that downward spiral, but her ex all the same.

"Inside me," she begged softly. "Please, Hudson. Just...for now. I need you."

My heart ached at the pain lacing her words, and what she wasn't saying.

This thing wouldn't be permanent. I got that from the desperation in her eyes. But I wanted her so damn bad that temporary would do.

For now.

I'd work on a future version of us after I cleaned the fear and tension and pain from her face, the shadows that lingered behind her eyes.

Before she crumpled on me, I worked my fingers through the knot on her towel, pulled her robe open and dipped my head to lick her breasts. Sucked on them. Marked her in ways that wouldn't easily fade.

She let me.

There's hope.

Her finger curled through my hair, tugging my head up.

"You want me to stop, princess?" I rolled her nipple between my thumb and forefinger until she moaned, and slid lower, kissing along her stomach. "Tell me to stop, Skye." *Before I fall head over fucking heels for you.*

Too late.

I watched her face as I licked her gushing hot slit, loving the way her hips rolled up with every touch. Her head flung back, and she knotted her hands in my hair, riding my face. My cock strained in my jeans, but now had to be about calming her, not satisfying a need that was never going to pass whether she let me fuck her now or any other time.

She was my girl. My one. My California and Texan hearts slammed together in my chest as her thighs clamped around my head. She came hard on my tongue, gushing hot cream on my lips. I cleaned her slowly, letting her come down and raised my head to find her fingers out of my hair and tangled in my own.

I raised them over her head gently, catching both with one hand. Hers were so much smaller, so fragile though I knew she'd hate to hear it.

"Is this okay?" I hesitated before crossing her wrists and pressing down to hold her in place while I worked on my belt.

"It is with you." I swore her eyes glowed as she gazed up at me, her lips parted.

"Fuck," I muttered, leaning down to kiss her hard and pinned her in place. "You tell me it's too much and I'll–"

"It's not. Promise, she whispered, reaching to touch me and guide my cock between her legs.

Her heat enveloped me and my groan answered hers as I slid inside her, not stopping until I was balls deep and aching to fill her with my seed.

"Don't promise what you can't control," I said roughly, slamming my hips down again and again.

She didn't fight me once, arching up to match me. Her heels dug into my ass as I worked her over, urging me deep, harder.

Rougher.

Sweat beaded between us as I obeyed, taking us to a place where no one else existed, where nothing could hurt her. And when she screamed into my chest she took me with her, her sweet pussy milking me endlessly.

I followed willingly to the woman I fell for back in a beach in another town and chased across the country for a second chance at love on a beach.

CHAPTER ELEVEN

SKYE

I curled on Hudson's chest, listening to his heart slow its frantic pace. My thighs were sticky, and he hadn't made an effort to clean me but I got it. And...I kinda of liked the marks he left on me, something I never liked from anyone else, and certainly not–

My eyes squeezed shut as I burrowed into his chest and let out a horrifyingly weak and pitiful sound.

"It's okay. He can't hurt you anymore. Promise." Hudson's finger stroking my hair never wavered.

"I know. I just hate that he still takes up space in my head."

"Want me to remove that for you?" Before I could take another breath I was on my back, staring up into the face of the man prepared to do anything to make me happy.

Little did he seem to know that he'd already done that–removed the threat to my existence that always hung over me.

When Archer gave me my assignment, I shook my head. "No. No fucking way. Sir,' I spat placing the folder back on his desk. "I won't be involved with him again."

"But you have asked to fix the problem he presented in the past. What changed?" Archer asked, ignoring the rejected case file.

"This is putting me right in with him. Rebuilding trust like what we had– that it was alright. This is far from okay."

Archer nodded, steeling his fingers. "You're right. It's not alright. Do you know how many women have died because of him? Indirectly, some," he ignored my gasp. "Others, because he tired of them, or they talked about his business. You thought he was bad, Skye, but the truth is he's trafficked women, drugs and ruined more lives than either of us can count on both hands. Are you prepared to let that slide?"

He held my gaze and I was the first to answer.

"No, sir. I'm not."

I kissed Hudson, snapping us both out of a place where we were lost in our heads and brought us back by complete accident. "I want a lot of things, Hudson, but I don't think I can have nice things." I offered him a sad smile. "Like you."

The best you'll get from me is a shitty partner who might fold at the worst time.

"What if I want something else?" Hudson wrapped me tight in his arms, tangling his legs around mine until I wasn't sure where he began, and I ended. "What if I think we're okay for more?"

His eyes begged me to give this a try and my traitorous heart ached to say *yes*.

"No." I shook my head. "Tonight can't happen again."

Hudson reared back, a hard look on his face. "You're right. It can't." He pushed back from me, leaving me in a pile of fake polyester bear fur, trembling a little from the force of our lovemaking.

Because Hudson didn't fuck No matter what he said, his sort of love started fun and got heavy fast. Really fast.

And I lived on a slow lane to solitude somewhere. Being caught up with him wasn't the best thing for either of us. And yet, I wanted him.

"Hudson?" I grabbed a crochet pink blanket—so,

so much pink–and wrapped it around myself. Not that it covered much, but that wasn't the point. "I'm sorry."

He laughed hollowly, raking a hand through his hair. "It should be me saying that to you." His hands trembled, his stance rigid, and I realized how much he'd hidden from me in order to take away my pain.

My heart melted a little.

Okay, a lot.

He paced the room, butt naked and incredible. The man's physique was beyond cut. He was powerful in every way, and none of the muscle was for decoration. I knew that now. Plus, the man had speed, determination, tenacity, love...what was I saying no to at this point?

His pacing grew agitated, his turns on the thick pile–yeah, pink–carpet leaving heavy indents as he stalked across the length of the room and back. It was the first time I'd seen him lose his shit, and I hated it. Wanted to fix him.

So I did the thing I thought he wanted most.

"Hudson, stop," I said quietly.

He spun on his heel, staring down at me with a hard, closed face. "You know I gave you everything. *Everything*, Skye. And my heart–fuck," he muttered rubbing his chest like he could remove the ache that tore him up from the inside.

I sympathized. Mine was the same.

"Come here," I whispered, unwrapping the blanket, and getting on my hands and knees to crawl to him. I kept it sexy, but I wanted him to see the lack of threat, what I was willing to put aside for him.

I had no idea how this would work; *if* it would work, but suddenly I saw what had been right in front of me the entire time and somehow missed it.

Missed *him*.

But he saw me when I needed him, and now I had to return that favour.

He knelt before me, hauled me up his body, frowning at me. "You shouldn't be down there."

"But it seemed like the right thing to do." I shrugged, looping my wrists behind his neck and settling over him.

Large hands caught my hips firmly and pulled me right into him, leaving no space between us. "Damn, you feel good, girl. You gonna give this thing a go? Or was that the last time I got to touch you like this?" he squeezed my ass, digging his fingers right in.

A breath whooshed from me, along with a mewl. I snapped my mouth shut and gave him a hard look. "No more freebies for you, fireboy."

"That's Ranger, princess. Just like you." He kissed me quick and drew back just as suddenly.

My heart thumped hard, and heat rose in my chest. "Do it again, but slower," I whispered. "And maybe we can find out just how long summer really lasts."

His smile turned sinful as he lifted me up and set me back down, right on top of the hard length that impaled me until I moaned his name against his mouth.

And then everything was long and slow for a damn long time.

I loved it. Him. Maybe that sort of love could cover a world of hurts, despite being so freaking scary. But with him I'd try it. Maybe for a real long time. He twirled the ring on my finger I forgot to take off, and gave me a hard squeeze.

"If I take this off now, it won't be long before it's back on," he promised darkly, before he began to move and I forgot all the arguments that could wait for the road trip back home to Texas.

Cliche? Maybe. But remember, ladies. If you've got a man who's willing to kneel for you, he thinks you're a queen.

Take that crown and be worthy of it. He'll never stop kneeling.

Thank you for reading

Thank you so much for reading!!
More than one easter egg from my Texan Devils
series floats around in Hudson and Skye's story, but
no Texas Rangers were harmed in the making of it...
at least, so far. This book runs concurrently with
RANGER'S STORM as the unit begins to undergo
a change of guard.
If you want to catch the whole series, start with
Andy and Ella's in my favorite second chance
romance of all time in RANGER'S WISH.
TEXAN DEVILS is also a crossover series with
RED HART RANCH.
Catch Archer in his own books:
SNOW ON THE RANGE (RHR book 1)

RANGER'S WRATH (TD book 5)
Mistletoe on the Range (forthcoming)

Spring Break With A Mafia Prince

a Rippton U/Love Beach morally gray new adult romance

CONTENT WARNING

This book contains themes often seen in both mafia and new adult morally gray romances. There is some light sword crossing, though this is not a major theme. Falcon refuses to apologize for his sexuality. This book also contains swearing, noir sex scenes, explicit sex scenes, heavy language and violence. The main female character is also untouched. Falcon doesn't apologize for that either, or what comes after.

Please read safety, and enjoy Falcon's time while he pretends to be anything but the mafia prince that he is.

CHAPTER ONE

FALCON

A haze of cigar smoke stained the internal guts of my multimillion dollar super yacht, the *Bella Vita*, while the girl who sucked my cock last night rode the capo's beside me this evening.

Huh. No accounting for taste.

Not that I'd have her back. I was a one-run man. My father's little tame mafia harem knew that while he visited—permanently—for this spring break tour their game had to be on. Afterward, they'd be tossed off the boat and I'd have my damn space back.

Not that my father and I saw eye to eye. Not after the way he'd treated my mother to the point she threw herself off the back of his last boat during a party years ago. He didn't even notice until hours later because he was too busy with some other cheap slut. Even so, I still had to play fucking nice with the Familia Don. Regardless, I had no interest in forming attachments of my own, despite the expectations I couldn't escape.

Not that there was a woman in this room who wasn't over used, over primped and over fucking everything.

Oh, wait. That last part was me.

This holiday was supposed to be my break away from Rippton U where I was surrounded with the same level of opulence and assholes, only there they were closer to my own age range.

My father's current party was full of has beens and wannabes who crowded around with the few loyal men who had his back. The few we both trusted. Maybe one or two untried.

One of those was Rose Drakehan, a capo in training. He had another title, but that would do for tonight. I'd mixed many substances for much else to make it through my exhausted mind.

Between the constant backstabbing, negotiations and betrayals of my father's world, all I wanted was a chance to get some literal sun and surf like the rest of the Rippton U contingent. Hell, even my cage fighting fuck up of a roomie was off getting his own ass tanned.

"*Sottocapo*," Bracchio, my father's man, bowed though his head didn't lower quite enough for my liking.

Mind, he ran my father's daily affairs while the title bestowed upon me was a...formality...for now. I'd take the mantle when the time came, probably enjoy it, even though it would come with the price of my father's life. He wouldn't abdicate his position as head of the Gianio Familia. That didn't make his smile any less sharp.

"Are you.... entertained enough this evening?"

I let my mouth curl into a sneer I felt all too much, even though the motion should have been wiped from my face. *My father would be appalled.*

But right now he was balls deep in the asshole of the discarded girl from last night, and I doubted that he neither saw nor cared.

Bile rose in my throat as I held the eyes of the man before me.

"I'm good. Thank you." My stilted speech belied my fatigue, my boredom at the entire nightly charade that often played out through into the day. "I need some air."

His smirk told me I'd shown a weak side to this man who would either report that to my father or capitalize on it, or both at some later date.

In the case of my father, as he finished his business with an animalistic groan, probably not that much later.

I pushed up from my seat, desperate for a breath of clean air, even if it was the salty sort that Love Beach provided that clung to my skin.

Anything was preferable to the brand of sin that etched itself to my bones in this cloistered place.

The religion of Gianio Familia.

And me it's heir.

I strode to the short ladder that led to the upper decks, all too conscious of the boat swaying beneath my feet, the constant thrum of the engine at idle, winding down for the night. As I reached the white fiberglass door that led to blessedly sea fresh air, a gentle hand pressed to my wrist from one side.

I stopped and looked into the shadows, though I didn't turn to face Rose Darkham. "Do you have a death wish, *ciccio*?" I asked in our native language.

He smiled slightly and shook his head. "You appeared...unsatisfied with tonight's entertainment. I know that the choices here are not always to your liking."

I matched his faint smile. "Smart observation."

More than once I had chosen a male play partner for the night over one of my father's female passed around companions. Neither my father nor his men cared, and I hadn't realized anyone took notice of my nocturnal habits other than my occasional playfellows.

Or that there was interest in becoming one of them.

"Is it?" Rose Darkham's rosebud mouth never changed its shape, but his eyes drifted over my body in an unbidden caress.

Light fingers brushed my thigh and when I didn't push him away immediately, my father's stray reached up boldly to cup my cock, squeezing me through my charcoal slacks. I gritted my teeth, biting my tongue to keep the moan that built in my throat on the inside.

The man, however young he seemed in comparison to the rest of my father's cadre, though he was probably only twenty something, maybe twenty-one or twenty-two like me, knew what to do with his hands. He gentled his touch on instinct when I didn't respond. Breath hissed between my teeth, though I managed to keep the volume down.

"No one here has earned the right to have their

hands on me tonight." I kept my voice aloof as I held his gaze and leaned into his space until we shared a single breath. "Until I give you permission, *ciccio*, keep your unworthy hands off me." I flicked out the tip of my tongue to brush his bottom lip to let a teasing edge filter into my words.

Why push him away when I might have a use for him later? Rose's head tipped back, and his eyes fluttered closed, that knowing touch dropping away. I swore the other man nearly came in his pants. The wave of power that washed over me was a heady thing.

I missed the contact when his hand left my cock almost immediately, but pushed my way through the door and forced my legs to mount the stairs one at a time until the brisk sea air wiped my head clear of the sinful, seductive air that was all too tempting below decks.

Any other night I might have taken him up on his offer. Tonight...I needed time to myself. Away from the mess my father made of his play time in an effort not to become my sire before my time was up.

You'll never escape your fate. One day you'll become what you hate.

The words my mother said to be the night before she left this life forever. I kept them with me always.

I might have to take my father's seat one day, but I didn't have to become him just yet.

I breached the haze that clung to me as I strode across the upper deck all the way to the stern. The few crewmen on clean up from our party time on this level before were long gone, leaving me alone with the sea and the stars for company despite being moored at the far end of Love Beach's Marina, away from the glitzy lights and tourist destinations.

It wasn't like we were the family friendly version of my spring break from Rippton U.

My pocket vibrated. I extracted my phone as I leaned over the railing at the back of the boat, the stillness beneath my feet a surprise after the constant moment and hum of the last days' travel. I lit the screen, smirking at my roommate's name.

Dex had his own share of troubles, but his not-girlfriend/Friday night fuck buddy wasn't anything he couldn't handle midweek.

DEX: Got kicked out of Zin's. All lonely. Come share my bed, bro.

DEX: You know I'm good for cuddles.

I nearly laughed outright at his bullshit. My thumb flew over the keypad in response.

FALCON: Keep yo sweaty ass outta my bed. I'm not taking Zinzi's slops.

DEX: Spoilsport.

FALCON: Just keeping it real, bro.

DEX: Yeah, sure. Maybe I'll steal whatever pretty piece you bring home next.

I snorted under my breath. Not likely; his soft spot was for one killer in knee high boots, dark denim, black hair and the attitude to take him on alone.

FALCON: Good luck with that, man. I'll watch from a front row seat.

DEX: Nothing to see here tonight, my friend.

FALCON: Grovel. It's what she needs to see and you know it.

DEX: I'll bend a knee to that woman any night, but she needs something I can't give her.

I nodded and pocketed my phone, knowing I'd have to top up my personal stash of whiskey when I got back to our room once he'd drunk himself dry. Zin needed space. He wanted to love bomb her, but in a good way—sort of. Shit, who was I kidding? They were toxic as fuck for each other but for whatever reason they also appeared to be what the other needed. She fought it. He didn't. Maybe he needed to fight her back.

I ignored the next spate of text messages that came through, knowing he'd have started in on what was probably my favorite bottle. It wasn't the first time I'd replaced it. Not that it mattered to me. I barely drank back on campus anymore.

The amount of liquor my father's crew stuffed into me on these trips to *harden me up* had the adverse effect of curing me of wanting the shit in my body for the rest of the semester. Half of me wanted to stay and look at who my father surrounded himself with; the other half couldn't wait for them to fucking leave.

I dropped my head into my hands with a groan and kicked at the railing. It reverberated against my arms, the vibrations ricocheting through my entire body. I scraped my nails through my scalp, relishing the light pain as a form of distraction.

"That kind of evening, huh?"

A soft, sweet voice that should never have been anywhere near my father or my boat brought my head up too fast. The blacked out horizon swam in a sea of stars that wouldn't stay put as I turned toward the girl who spoke to me like I hadn't nearly just puked my guts into the ocean below me a moment before anyway.

A vision in a pale blue, cotton dress with thin straps and a sweetheart neckline that stopped at her mid-calf, my body's reaction to her hit me somewhere around the chest region. Dirty blonde hair that curled in a light wave around her throat and tumbled down her bare back shifted gently in the night's breeze that I hadn't noticed in my bid to escape my father's lair. Hell, she could have been there the whole time and I might not have noticed her.

How the hell did I miss her standing there?

The thought made me illogically angry, but before I could rein my temper in, the words I didn't want to say flew out.

"What are you doing here?" I snapped, and winced. *Fuck, I sound like my father.*

The girl watched me quietly. Anyone else might have taken a step back. Anyone else might have run like hell when I glowered at him like I just did with her.

Anyone who knew my name. Which was when it hit me.

She has no idea who I am.

CHAPTER TWO

FALCON

I took a second glance at myself. Charcoal pants, white shirt, half unbuttoned, hair a mess from rubbing my hands through it a second ago. And I hadn't shaved in days. Hell, I probably looked like any random college aged kid out for a joyride.

"Sorry, that was—"

"Rude," she reprimanded me gently. "It's okay. We all have those nights. I think my father is having one right now." My mystery girl, who had be college-age, like me, tilted her head toward the stairs I came up a few minutes before.

Raised voices emanated from behind the door I'd shut.

"Ah." My father mentioned a late meeting. *No*

wonder he finished up with the slut so fast. "Did you just arrive?" A single nod. Not once did her eyes turn wary. "Mmm." I rubbed a hand over my chin, the not so short bristles biting into my palm. "And you have no one else with you here? Just your father?" I winced as something banged below. Not a gunshot, but her father wasn't the only one having a shit night.

"Just me," she said softly, standing there in that thin blue cotton sundress long after the evening set in.

And the night breeze which wasn't so gentle in spring. The long hem drifted around her slim calves, her hands twitching like she might wrap her arms around herself, but she didn't shift under my gaze.

It took me less than half a second to make the decision.

"Where are you staying?"

"We have a house behind the town. It's not far, just enough away from...everything." she shrugged.

I nodded; I got it, not wanting to be in the middle of the tourist destination of Love Beach. "Within walking distance?"

"If you're used to walking."

"Campus is fairly huge. I'm on spring break. Wait here for a minute?" I asked.

Hell, that was new. I didn't ask anyone for anything.

The girl nodded again, and didn't move. The single movement gave me the impression that she was used to waiting on other people to get their business done before anyone thought of her.

I rolled my lips inward on that thought, still watching her face as I backed up a few steps and mimicked her nod. "I'll be back in a second."

I turned on my heel and jogged forward, toward the bow of the boat, not willing to head lower toward my room. I'd left a zip up hoodie on the bridge earlier in the day where the captain resumed an old lesson in teaching me how to read nautical charts. For whatever reason, I loved studying the damn things, and he was more than willing to share an old passion with an eager student.

"You didn't move." I found the girl standing exactly where I left her.

She looked up at me curiously. "You did say not to."

I frowned down at her, realizing she stood just half a foot shorter than my six foot one inches. "Do you always do what strange men tell you to do?"

"This would be the first time." One lean shoulder lifted in a shrug and fell.

I watched the motion and swallowed, the swell of anger blooming fresh. "And if I'd been coming back with the intent to hurt you?" I said, managing to keep my voice soft, squeezing the hoodie in my hands.

"Were you?" She frowned up at me, and suddenly I hated how that looked on her.

"No." I held out the hoodie. "Let me walk you home. Away from this. You shouldn't be here anyway. And it'll get colder later. More than this, from what I've seen of the nights so far."

She contemplated me for a long moment, and just as I thought she would refuse my offer, she slipped one arm into the hoodie that was miles too freaking big for her. Letting me wind the soft, grey material around her slim frame that seemed too delicate to be here, near me, near anything of my family's before something—or one of us—broke her, she turned in a semi-circle until I completed the job.

Suddenly I stood in front of her, unsure how we got here as I fiddled with the zip and secured her into my jacket, rolling the sleeves up her wrists a few turns.

"Better?"

"Thank you." She bit her lip and *finally* wrapped

her arms around herself like I'd guessed she had wanted to do before. "It's much warmer."

"Yeah." Fuck her father for letting her walk out of the damn house and into a meeting with her dressed like that. She looked like bait, for fuck's sake. "Come on. Show me how you get home. We just arrived yesterday, and I don't know this place yet."

"I'll be your tour guide." She still didn't move.

I waited, my palms itching and then I broke every damn rule I had for myself and held out my hand. "Show me...I don't know your name," I murmured.

"Bella."

I rocked back on my heels, a smile forming on my face. "Just like the boat," I muttered. Her expression morphed into confusion. I waved the comment away. "It's nothing." It wasn't. "My boat is also called Bella. *The Bella Vita,* a beautiful life."

I tugged on the hand she gave me, pulling her closer to me. My chest closed. With any other woman I'd already know exactly what I wanted to do with her—hell, that was an outright lie. Any other woman I'd already have in my bed. Over the railing, on the nearest furniture...

Another lie.

I was getting good at those tonight.

I knew exactly what I wanted to do with Bella tonight. I wanted to walk her home, make sure she stayed warm and see her safe inside her home. And then get my ass back here and find out what business her father had with mine.

But her sapphire blue eyes that mirrored the dark water that lapped at the boat drew me out of my head, in a way that no one else I knew could achieve.

"You know my name," she whispered, seeming to lose her nerve.

I smiled faintly. "Falcon Gianio. Walk with me, Bella?"

She let me draw her off my boat, away from my father and hers, and onto unmoving land. My hand was still wrapped around hers. Bella's steps were much shorter than mine and even though this was a girl I had just met, a girl who I knew nothing about, I didn't want to let her go.

Me, the mafia prince who hated contact with another person unless I was about to end up balls deep in their soft, warm flesh.

But that wasn't on tonight's menu. Not in the least. Whatever the hell this was, I had no intention of fucking my woes out into Bella's soft, pale body. Her hand trembled in my grip and I loosened my hold instantly.

"Am I hurting you?" *Am I scaring you? Too much for you?* Fuck, I was freaking myself out as much as I probably terrified her.

"No," she whispered, pulling her hand away. I missed the contact as she pushed her hair back from her face and made a messy but cute as all fuck knot with its dirty blonde strands at her nape. "I just...I worry about my father."

I let out a short laugh, softening my tone belatedly when she glanced sideways at me. "He's with my father and while mine's in a mood, he isn't in *that* sort of a mood." I took the elastic from her hand when she paused, biting her lip again. "I've scared you."

"No." She shook her head as I picked out the curls she knotted up and unwound the mess at her nape, winding her hair into a twist, and looping the elastic around it twice. "Oh, alright, yes. You did. A bit. I don't understand any of this," she confessed, wrapping her arms so tight around herself that she seemed to shrink. "Thank you." One hand pressed to her hair. "How did you learn to do that?"

"I used to do it for my mother. She had long, dark hair, and it used to knot on the boat—not mine, my father's, then, he sold it, afterward." I stopped talking and took a breath. "She taught me to put it up for her."

"Is she around tonight?" Bella glanced backward along the jetty.

My throat tightened. "No. She's...not with us anymore."

"I'm sorry, Falcon." Her hand brushed the back of mine, and I automatically sought her out again, securing her in a firm grip. She didn't pull away. "I lost my mother to cancer three years ago. That was when my father...he also struggles," she whispered.

I nodded, tugging her close to my side as we walked along the jetty and the boardwalk that skirted around the edge of the town, following the beach that was almost deserted at close to midnight.

"He shouldn't have brought you with him tonight," I said tightly. "That boat is no place for someone like you."

"Too plain," she murmured, looking down at the ground and I realized for the first time she was barefoot.

Somehow, that made her all the more sexier, but now I was worried about her damn well hurting her feet.

"Too innocent," I said abruptly as she turned and led me up a hill away from the town onto a rocky path. I stopped and bent at my knees. "Climb on, Bella. You're not walking barefoot all the way up there."

"I made it down." Her palm pressed lightly to my back as she considered my offer.

I groaned, playing it up, though my thighs did actually ache in that position. "Come on, I'm an old man here. Do me a favor, yeah?"

She slapped at me even as she giggled, and let me hoist her onto my back. Slim legs—almost too slim— linked around my waist as she looped her arms around my neck. Hell, the girl weighed almost nothing at all.

"Fuck it, I'm feeding you tomorrow," I muttered under my breath.

"Hmm?" She rested her chin on my shoulder.

The scent of berries assaulted me from behind. I closed my eyes and suppressed a groan at the freshness of her right mother fucking *there* pressed against me. Squeezing one calf muscle and resisting the urge to run my hands up and down her legs, I took the hill at a run, needing to burn some of my excess energy off before I did something we'd both regret.

"Turn," she said a little breathlessly when we hit a street corner. "That one." Bella pointed across the road a white and gray painted three story beach vacationer house complete with a stilted lower level and all the windows and verandas a house could ever need.

I stopped outside its stairs, looking up and up as I let her down gently. "It's just you and your dad in here?"

"He owns it." I heard the shrug in her voice before I turned back to her, sliding my hands automatically to encircle her waist.

Her eyes flared wide in the reflected street light, an awareness passing between us. I swallowed and dropped my hands, but the damage was already done.

"I'm sorry, I shouldn't have—"

She rose gracefully onto her bare toes and grazed her lips across my cheek. "Thank you for walking me home," she whispered, her lips still near mine.

It didn't take a half second's thought to catch her chin gently between my fingers and turn my head to brush my mouth across hers.

Bella's stuttered breath matched my heartbeat that slammed once into my chest at full tilt, then stilled.

And I stepped back.

"I'd do it again," I murmured, unsure which part

I meant, the walk or the kiss. Or both. Space gave me clarity, and my heartbeat resumed its normal path.

"Let me give this back to you." She struggled with the zip on my jacket and though it was in me to watch her fight it, I closed my hand over hers and squeezed instead.

"Keep it. Besides, I want to take you out tomorrow."

The hell did that come from?

Her eyes widened like they had a second before when I kissed her.

A kiss I wasn't going to think about because with anyone else I would have pushed her back against the house, forced her mouth open with my tongue, and left her wet and mewling there on the front doormat.

With this girl—I ached to beg her permission to kiss her again, fucking *earn it*. If she'd let me.

Bella nodded. "Alright," she whispered. "What did you have in mind?"

"I have a smaller boat. If you don't get seasick?"

She shook her head. "I'm good."

I grinned. "Easy, then. Come by the jetty tomorrow morning. Early as you like. I'll be up."

"And here I thought you sounded like a party

boy." The sort of smile I wanted to kiss from her soft lips turned up at the corners.

I tried not to stare, but I knew I'd fall asleep to that memory tonight. Maybe another night if not tonight.

"I can be," I said carefully, not wanting to lie outright. "But to be honest, I don't enjoy it. Not always. With the boys back on campus, yeah, we can get loud," I admitted.

"Sounds like fun." She smiled, and I actually rocked back a step.

"Yeah. But you, Bella, I will see tomorrow. If you want?" There I went, asking questions again.

"I want," she murmured.

"Good. Now go inside so I can see that I didn't run all the way up that hill for no reason," I growled, swatting at her in play.

Alright, half in play because if I'd caught her when she giggled and managed to evade me, that jacket zipped between us wouldn't have meant shit.

But giggle she did, and she ran up those two flights of stairs without me accosting her. I waited at the bottom until I heard her keys in the lock, and the light flicked on three stories above ground level.

"I'm safe. You can go to sleep now, Falcon," she called down softly.

Not that there would be a neighbor awake to hear our little tête-à-tête.

I grinned and waved, shoving my hands into my pockets and headed back down the hill to plan tomorrow out. No part of me wanted to leave her alone tonight, and every inch of me craved to break her window open, crawl through and do terrible things with her in the dark.

Ruin the innocence that exuded from her pores. But that wasn't who Bella was and...

Who I could be with her.

The chance to be someone more than the Don of the Gianio Familia's son. Someone who didn't have to worry about the underhand deals my father made tonight or what might come back to bite him tomorrow. Or spill his blood come daybreak.

Tomorrow, I could steal a single day with her, let everything go and pretend—for twelve fucking hours —not to think about who I might have to be come sunset.

Just for one damn day.

I shoved my hands into my pockets as I headed away from the house, back to the boat where my father waited, along with hers. Screw them both. I had a date to plan.

Plus, it was damn cute that she thought I'd sleep between now and seeing her again.

CHAPTER THREE

BELLA

"Where are you going?" Neil Lawrence's eyes had deeper, darker circles beneath them than any other day this week, or this year, though I'd become used to his not so new nocturnal habits. I didn't know what time my father came in last night, and I had learned not to ask.

Keep quiet, don't say anything. Don't rock the boat.

Cute, considering my destination for the day.

"I'm going sailing."

He frowned at me. "You're not a sea girl."

"Nope. And you're not a night owl." I kissed his cheek. "Bye, Dad. Will you be home tonight?"

He shrugged one tired shoulder. "I don't know." The kind of helplessness that rolled off him stung.

I dithered at the front door to the beach house on the hill where I could see most of Love Beach that we had owned most of my life. "Do you want me to stay?"

His mouth twitched. "No, Bella. Have fun. Who are you—"

The doorbell rang, and I nearly left the mortal plane.

I opened the door, cussing in my head, though I stopped when I saw his shadow hovering just on the other side.

"I left some of my years behind thanks to you," I informed Falcon. "You told me to find you at the marina."

He had the grace to look abashed, and it was cute as hell on his carved face, the dark brows and hair, his arched lips and olive skin. Something told me this man was not anywhere near as innocent as he seemed—I knew who his father was, after all—but Falcon had proved to be nothing but sweet in the short time I'd known him.

I refused to judge him by the actions of his family's reputation rather than his own.

"This is your date?" My father broke into my reverie.

"Yes. This is—"

"Falcon Gianio." Falcon grinned and extended his hand.

I blinked. Somehow, I expected something to pass between them, seeing as we met on his boat the night before, but Falcon didn't hold back, clasping my father's hand firmly.

Dad looked slightly mollified. "And you know how to sail?"

"Yes, sir. The captain gave me a refresher course, but I've failed many times. I used to race maxi yachts a few years back, actually."

"No kidding?" Dad slipped his hands into his pockets, looking between us. "Alright, then. Not too late, and call me if you need me. I'll be..." Dad nodded toward the study.

I bit my lip, wishing I would say something but also knowing I wouldn't. Work kept him busy, and not thinking about Mom. Or her absence. "I know. I'll be safe." I reached back blindly, my fingers extended.

Falcon's hand closed firmly around mine. "She'll be back at a reasonable time, sir. Good weather all day. I checked twice."

"Neil. And that's good to know." Dad's shoulders relaxed a fraction more. "I'll see you later." He leaned over and kissed my cheek, squeezing my shoulder and wandered off to the other end of the house.

I watched him leave, itching to follow, to say something, but what? We lost Mom years ago, and his grief had never matched up with mine. Besides, it wasn't fair of me to ask him to put a hold on his life to remember her.

"Ready?" Falcon traced his fingers through my hair, tucking a few strands behind my ear.

I nodded, suddenly keen to leave the house. "Yes. I am."

"Good." He pressed a kiss to my temple that jolted me with its familiarity and the secure presence of him as he drew me out of the house and down to the marina.

"Feel better?" Falcon ran his knuckles across my shoulders.

I suppressed a shiver as I looked over my shoulder at him, trying not to strangle the boat's steering wheel — excuse me, the helm. I was still getting used to the language that flowed so easily from him, and was well out of my depths. But as before, Falcon didn't make me feel stupid or insignificant about not knowing something.

Rather, his passion shone through as he showed me how to steer and to use the little tails in the equally small clear panel in the sail spread wide above me to gauge the wind and when to tack.

I had the impression I'd never conquer that last part. My first attempt left us stalled in the water while he howled with laughter, set us back up and had me try again. My second attempt actually caught the wind, and I was determined to keep those little tails in their square, flying.

Mind, with the way he couldn't seem to stop from touching me, that made concentrating a hard call.

We left from the marina early in the morning but that had been hours ago. He had charts out, and we were headed for the lee side of a small island I remembered hearing about ages ago that the kids often used to ride out to when I was younger to go swimming. I was never allowed to go when they did and by the time I came back the next summer, those same kids seemed to have formed friendships I never broke into after that.

"You're doing amazing." Falcon resting his hands on my hips, his thumbs turning small circles over my white denim capri pants. "Are you sure this is your first time?"

"On any boat that wasn't attached to the jetty by a strong rope," I reassured him. "Your instructional technique is good."

"Or you listen well." He leaned down, his lips brushing the skin just below my ear.

I shivered, unable to hold that back, and his soft laughter afterward doubled down on the action.

His hands closed on my hips tight then let go, a breath shuddering out of him as he stepped back, creating distance between us. I missed him straight away, aching for him, but the way his breath came hard at my back...I wasn't game to turn around to confront him.

Finally, he cleared his throat. "See the island? That's our destination." His hand covered mine on the helm. "Mind if I take it from here?"

I relinquish the wheel, cramping my hands. "Please," I smiled. "That was fun but...don't rely on me to do anything technical."

"You're much better than you think." Falcon watched the little window above us, then glanced around as the island came in closer, his brow knitting as he sought a particular spot. "There."

The next minutes were a rush as he pulled the sail in, working like a one man army hell bent on total efficiency.

I had no idea what he saw, but he clearly did as the anchor went down with a tremendous *thunk*. He threw the boat into reverse and once the anchor dragged and grabbed, he stopped and we floated in a wide circle just off the island in the still deep water.

Everything around us, except for a few birds and the wind, was silent.

"That was impressive." I gripped the glossy railing, watching the small white caps lap at the rocks a hundred yards away. "You read the water like others do a road."

"I had a master give me his best cheat sheet last night after I left you." His chest brushed my back as he slid his hands around my stomach. "And his grandson leant me his boat this morning after I promised to let him teach me to fish."

I giggled. "You, fish?" I tipped my head back, resting against his shoulders. Flacon let me, his body a wall of strength that felt so good when I could just let everything go. "Do you want to learn how to fish?"

"Not at all." His grimace filtered through his voice as he caught my chin in his fingertips and tipped my head back a little more. "Right now, though..." He leaned down enough to brush his mouth over mine once, then again. "I'd like to feed you."

"Not what a girl wants to hear," I muttered.

He laughed at me, not letting go just yet. "Let me have my way," he cajoled. "At least for now."

"Somehow I suspect you're rather good at that." I let him manhandle me to a soft cream leather bench seat that lined both sides of the small cockpit.

"And I thought you hadn't noticed." Falcon disappeared down the small hatch that led to the inside of the sailing yacht with a small kitchenette and a few long berths plus a tiny bathroom I was inherently grateful for, and reappeared holding a tray of salad and chicken rolls plus a bottle of white wine. "Tada da."

"You've been busy." I reached down and liberated everything from his, reveling in the shock on his face. "Doesn't anyone help out where you're from?"

He quickly schooled the emotion off his face and back into the semblance of the easy going persona I'd come to associate with him. "Not the— thanks," he murmured, running his fingers along my arm.

Falcon climbed one handed back onto the deck and helped unload the burden onto the fold out glossy wooden table that magically appeared from the other side of the helm.

"He loves this boat. The boy you borrowed it from." I tidied a small corner of his things to make room for the platter that followed.

"He's a few years older than me, so not a boy, to be fair." He shot me a sideways amused glance. "What makes you say that?"

I took a roll off the plate and filled it with salad and some pulled chicken. "Look at how well the boat is varnished, or whatever you call it. There isn't a mark on it. That's care and love and a whole lot of hours."

Flacon stilled. "You see a lot."

I shrugged. "It's kind of obvious, I guess?"

"Perhaps." He settled next to me. "We see the world through a different filter."

I ate for a moment before I realized he just sat there, his own lunch untouched, watching me eat. After a moment I put my roll down and cleared my throat. "Do I have something stuck in my teeth?"

He started. "Huh? Not at all."

I nudged him gently. "It's weird eating alone with you staring at me like a creeper," I whispered.

Falcon stared at me, then laughed so loudly he scared birds perched on a rock a few dozen yards away. "Hell, girl." He draped an arm across the back of the seat and tipped his head back. "I haven't laughed like that since I left campus."

"When was that?"

"Last week."

I rolled my lips inward. Anyone else might be horrified at that statement, but I got it. Besides, I didn't want to call him out on a lifestyle I doubted he could control if his family was anything like mine. "What are you studying?"

"Economics." He toyed with my hair. "What about you? Are..."

"Art history. It's a family business. But also, I love it." I shrugged, all too used to hearing why my choices were poor.

"Sounds magical."

"It's dry." I laughed. "You know, you wanted to feed me but that's a door that goes both ways. Eat." I lifted his roll and wiggled it.

Both eyebrows raised. "Where I'm from—" He broke off for the second—or was that the third time—this morning.

I mirrored his eyebrows. "Doesn't that give you a headache after a while? You're gonna need Botox.

Where you're from, what? Doesn't anyone dare challenge The All Great and Mighty Falcon Gianio?" I teased.

He snored. "Hell, no. You don't want to find out what happens to the ones who do," he muttered, despite the way his smile curved up at one side. He took a bite of his roll, regardless.

We finished our rolls in silence, and I sipped at the small glass of wine he poured for both of us afterward, when he wouldn't let me help clean up.

I knew he meant it. I knew exactly who he was when I met him the night before. Dad talked about all of them, warning me away from the group below which was why I was left on the deck after he checked there was no one left wandering around with assurances I'd be safe, if somewhat frozen.

A shiver rippled over me. I reached for Falcon's jacket I'd left on the seat beside me in the sunshine. His hand on my wrist stopped me.

"Cold?" he murmured, sliding his other arm across my back. I nodded and he tucked me into his side, resting his chin on the top of my head. Warmth pervaded me, sinking bone deep. Deeper than the fluffy material ever could. "I wish we could stay here like this." He stroked my arm gently in time with the sway of the boat.

"We can't." I hated that I said anything and shut my mouth fast.

Stupid, stupid.

It sounded ungrateful, and he'd been so sweet, saving me from a day of worrying after Dad, who would have told me to leave him alone in the nicest terms anyway.

Just another solitary day wandering about Love Beach. The perfect place to be the loneliest person in the world.

"Lost you there." His touch grazed my cheek as he tipped my head back to rest against his shoulder.

Warm breath brushed my lips. "Sorry." I bit my lip. "I—"

"You don't need to apologize to me, Bella. Ever." He shifted so we faced each other, though he still held me close.

My eyes drifted shut. I didn't want to have this conversation. Despite being up close and personal with Falcon Gianio's stunning, carved face, I blocked him out. *Okay,* I started to say, but his mouth pressed gently to mine, warm and open, in the lightest, noninvasive kiss possible.

Breath caught in my throat. We stayed like that for the longest moment, his hand curved around my cheek, stealing warmth from each other. Slowly our lips parted. He drew back like he had the night before, and the smallest sound left my lips.

Don't stop like that. I wanted to say it, but I couldn't, and tipped my chin down to hide my disappointment. As always, I was unwilling to push into that space where if I did something wrong, he could reject me and that would hurt twice as much.

The soft growl reverberated through his chest where my hand rested, toying with the buttons on his shirt, breaking me out of my headspace.

"Don't do that, Bella," he murmured, the lightest warning note in his voice.

"Do what?" I couldn't look at him, my cheeks blazing. *What did I do wrong?*

"Don't hide from me. You are beautiful, just like your name." His hold drew my chin back up. I reluctantly met his gaze. "If you want something from me, say so."

My mouth dried. "I don't— I mean, I can't—"

I stumbled over every word, stuttering just like six-year-old me used to do when I was shoved on stage at school and ended up running off crying because I couldn't remember the words. The spotlight had never been my favorite place.

His gaze searched my face, and softened a little.

"Tell me to stop if you don't like something. I'll go slow. Can you do that part?" He frowned a little.

I nodded. "I can do that."

"Good girl." He tucked his hands around me, winding his fingers in my hair, and settled his mouth over mine again. The gentlest pressure in a sweet kiss.

But this time, he didn't pull away.

CHAPTER FOUR

FALCON

Bella made the sweetest sound when I covered her mouth with mine and ran my tongue across her bottom lip. The urge to force my way inside her wet heat, push her back and make her moan beneath me prickled at my skin in an overwhelming wave of arousal.

I shoved that selfish need back, and did what I promised her, taking it slow.

Even if it fucking killed me.

Hell, she'd made me laugh, more than once. She deserved the reward she'd earned.

When Bella's soft lips parted I groaned into her

mouth, pulling her closer as I tangled my fingers into her hair, massaging her scalp and struggled to hold to my own promise.

"Falcon," she murmured, breaking the kiss briefly to push her body against me in a need to be closer.

I swallowed hard, needing the same thing, just without all the damn denim and cotton in the way. When she went for my jacket earlier, I couldn't stand the thought of one more damn layer of clothing between me and her.

I held to my resolve—motherfucking just—and slid my tongue alongside hers gently enough to draw a mewl from her. My heart slammed into my ribs but I kept her close, kissing her slow like I promised. Her tongue flicked against mine, the lightest touch and I swore I'd explode in my pants if she did it more than once.

Which proved to not be true at all, just a test of my resolve and utter luck as she tormented me with those tiny flicks, her nails scratching lightly at my chest as her fingers curled like a kitten's on my shirt. Her breath came in short pants at first, but she settled into a rhythm, her body softening into my embrace as my suspicions grew.

When I eased her back onto the leather bench seat, tucking my jacket beneath her head like a pillow—*knew that would come in handy*—I skated one hand down to her hip and squeezed. Just gently, but the way she bucked into me before I settled my weight over her, and how her eyes flew open, widening in stunned, fresh arousal, told me everything.

"Too much?" I asked softly, watching her face.

"Ah, a little–" she stuttered, her words breaking off

I swore that on anyone else her stammer wouldn't be so freaking cute. On her...I leaned down and kissed her deeply until all the tension I'd intentionally put back into her melted away. Her sigh when I settled my weight over her hit me somewhere deep around chest height. I slid a hand along her body, curved my fingers over her thigh and pulled her leg out a little.

Enough that I could sink into the spot between. The heat of her emanated through her white denim pants. I released a shuddering breath and tried not to grind into her, but there'd be no hiding how aroused I was at this proximity. Which was the point.

I expected her to stiffen and push me away. Hell,

I expected a slap for pushing her, after she'd barely been able to speak to me before. For a girl who could sass me out and tease me like she did, when it came to intimacy, she was painfully shy and beyond inexperienced.

My kisses grew rougher and I drew back, needing to keep everything light and easy for her. Fuck, I didn't want to break this sweet girl I'd just found who had come to represent everything that I didn't have in my world that I wanted so badly it hurt.

Just one day. That's all I want.

Sucking in a deep breath through her nose, she kissed me back and hooked her leg around the back of my knee. The move was awkward, but she raised her hips and pressed back into me, stealing my sanity at the implied contact. I grazed my hand along her ribs, holding her in place.

Breaking the kiss, I didn't speak at first, my mind whirling. She watched me, her breaths slow and easy, eyes dozy as all fuck with arousal. I stroked my thumb across her bottom lip, loving how plump and red stained they'd become with our kisses.

She wiggled a little, testing me further, though I doubted she had any idea what she was doing.

Deciding to push the boundaries a little myself I

feathered kisses along her jaw and across her throat, licking and sucking on all the spots where I thought she might be the most sensitive. My hands went on a tour of their own, grazing the pads of my fingers around the swell of her breasts, the undersides where I thought she might ache the most without touching the sensitive peaks.

No way was I giving her pleasure that easy. I'd teach her, if that's what she wanted, but she'd also learn to ask, with me.

And I'd enjoy that part the most.

"Ohh," she whispered, eyes lust drunk, flaring wide before her heavy lids dropped back again, almost shuttering on me.

"Nu uh." I shook my head, coming back to press a firm kiss to her lips to wake her up. "Don't you drop out on me, Bella. I want all your attention right here. And I want to touch you more. Can I?" A loaded question that involved clothes, or the lack of them.

She'd get there with me in a second.

"Y– yes." The second half came out surprisingly clear. Her gaze met mine through thick lashes, head on and challenging. "Please, Falcon."

Fuck. Me.

I wasn't completely sure of what she just asked me, but hell, was I here for it.

I closed my hand gently around her breast through her tee, squeezing rhythmically and working the motion toward her nipple. Her breath came in fast pants until I squeezed the tight nub through her thin, lacy bra beneath, then, holding her eyes, I pushed her shirt up, and licked my way toward her breast.

Her torn cry when I latched onto her nipple over the soft lace made me inherently relieved that I'd taken her well away from everyone else for the day.

Because those sounds were mine, and no one else's.

"Have you done this before, Bella?" I murmured, feeling only slightly predatory.

"Yes, once," she whispered.

"Good. I'll get his name later," I muttered, needing to tear someone apart.

Her laugh tore at me in both good and terrible ways. "Stop that."

She swatted at my hair, then slid her fingers through the dark waves, sighing when I suckled on her again. Her hips rocked against me and I swallowed hard, teasing her nipple with my tongue until she arched and cried out again.

I slid a hand over her stomach, pressing her flat to

the leather beneath, and rubbed my fingertips just beneath the waistband on her pants. "Here?"

"Nu uh—" The sound she made wasn't really a word at all. More a stolen breath that burst the moment it expelled from her lips.

"Is that a no, Bella? How many men to do I need to find?" I growled playfully.

Alright, so not so playfully, but she wriggled beneath me, giggling all the same. Fuck, she had to know I meant it. Right? *Right?*

"No others," she admitted in a small voice, like she expected me to abandon her on the spot.

Fuck, with my reputation, I didn't blame her in the least. It didn't take a genius to guess that she'd checked up on my name the night before, or this morning. Or talked to her father about me. Hell, I never did make it back to see what my sire wanted with hers.

But that conversation could wait

"No others, hmm?" I toyed with the soft strip of flesh over her belly. She might be tiny but she still had curves in the right places to squeeze and suck on. "Do you want me to stop, *bella*?" I made her name the term of endearment this time, and her eyes flared wide with recognition as I pitched my voice low.

"Not yet," she whispered back.

I nodded my approval, flicking the button open on her pants to show my intent, still playing with her breast with my other hand. She whimpered prettily when I toyed with her, tracing my fingers over her clothes, then plunged my hand inside her panties.

And encountered bare, damp flesh.

A deep sound reverberated in my chest. Even I didn't know if I meant it in praise or dissatisfaction. "Have you been lying to me, Bella?" I slid my fingers through her slick, naked folds as she arched and trembled beneath me.

"N– no," she managed, shaking all fucking over. "I've never—"

"Never what?" I teased my fingertips at her entrance, the heel of my hand pressed to her clit, never having intended to go this far today. I'd wanted to see what she'd do when I touched her, but finding her waxed, perfectly tender flesh beneath those normal clothes broke me. "You can't pretend not to have been touched before and then I find out you're all wet and smooth right here. That doesn't add up." I kept my voice low and soft, knowing the threat was that much worse than if I lost my temper outwardly.

Inside, I seethed. Had she lied to me? If she had — fuck, she put on a good show. I'd been completely convinced by what I assumed was the truth at face value. Now? I swallowed and pressed a finger inward.

Her thighs tightened, clamping around my hand. "Stop!" she cried.

I froze in place at the pure panic etched in the hard lines carved across her otherwise soft, dozy face. *There's no faking that.*

Not moving, I leaned down and kissed her gently. "Talk to me, Bella." I nudged her cheek with my nose. "Tell me all your secrets."

She shook her head, a bright stain flushing her pale cheeks even as heat enveloped my hand.

Well, well.

I started to withdraw my hand when she squeezed her eyes shut, then threw them open and stared at me with that same flaring brand of defiance that was all her she'd shown me before.

"I'm a virgin," she blurted, still trembling all over. Just...lesser than before.

"I guessed as much," I said dryly.

She frowned at me. "Then what was that?" She looked pointedly at my hand still inside her pants.

It was my turn to blush. "Ah. I— dammit, girl. I like bald pussies," I muttered, pulling away.

She surprised me again, catching my wrist. "N– not yet," she mumbled.

The stutter was back. But then, I had wanted her to ask me for what she wanted.

"Tell me what you want," I prompted softly, pressing my fingertips rhythmically into her soft, slicked flesh.

"I want— oh, fuck, Falcon," she gasped, lifting her hips when I rubbed her gently without pushing my fingers into her.

"I know, beautiful," I stroked her until her breath caught, finding that sweetly painful edge but also knowing that without touching her clit or pushing my fingers inside her, she probably couldn't climax. Though from the different sort of flush climbing her cheeks, it was a damn close thing. "Tell me," I cooed, teasing myself as much as I did her.

My cock thickened and strained against my jeans, but I focused on her face, her short, shattered breaths that brushed my lips when I dipped my head to steal more kisses.

"I can't think when you do that." She stared at me, her legs falling open so beautifully for me.

"I know, I don't play fair." I kept stroking her. "Fuck, you're wet. Let me taste you," I murmured, dragging my tongue across her bottom lip.

I'd been wrong. It didn't take my touch to make her come. Just my words.

She cried out as she spasmed under my fingers. Heat gushed around me and I knew she'd be dripping by the time I got her clothing off to clean her with my tongue.

I kissed her through the remainder of her orgasm, her smooth pussy pulsing against my fingers. I'd given myself the world's biggest fucking tease in making her come unintentionally without having my fingers inside her. Neither of us took that pleasure though she did in a different way.

Slowly, the tremors that wracked her subsided. I held her close, rocking my hips into her as I withdrew my hand to her whimpers and sucked her scent from them.

She watched, fascinated as I finished then rubbed the last of her own flavor over her lips. She licked the residue up obediently, her eyes curious. She never backed down and I nearly disgraced myself like a schoolboy rubbing up against her obsessively.

Sucking in my own deep breath, I slid down her body, taking her pants with me. She didn't object, letting me undress her, until I tugged her shoes and the white denim from her body, as well as her lace panties that matched the lacy bra.

Her hands fluttered at her sides. I caught one,

kissing her knuckles hard. Her fingers closed around mine, belying her anxiety. I didn't let go as I settled between her thighs, anchoring one knee over my shoulders, and dipped my head to my task.

Her skin, already swollen and glistening, left me aching with need as I licked her gently. Flattening my tongue, I cleaned her first before I brought her next orgasm on. She mewled above me, her fingers digging into the back of my hand as her thigh flexed over my shoulder. The scent of her drove me mad with need, so sweet and salty and clean. *Perfect for us.* I lapped at her, savoring the taste I memorized for later when I wasn't with her.

My cock ached to drive inside her sweet center, but I teased her tight hole with my tongue instead, soothing her flesh until she shivered for me. Then I plunged my tongue inside her, enjoying her squeal way too fucking much as she rocked against my face. Nails clawed in my hair at the deluge of sensations I knew she hadn't felt from coming on someone's face before.

Her hips raised, bucking into me. I untangled our hands, pressing my palm flat to her belly to hold her down and pulled her thigh open to me. Bella gasped shuddering breaths in as I left her exposed, and licked my way up to her clit, sucking her bundle of nerves into my mouth. It only took a few flicks before she screamed, arching where I pinned her down.

The sound that left me was feral. I was halfway up her body before my brain caught up with the message that we weren't fucking her today.

She's unbroken and not ruined and a fucking virgin.

And she's *mine*.

Bella's arms launched around my neck, her mouth crashing into mine in the first full kiss she'd initiated. I caught her against me, lowering us both back to the bench seat as she tasted herself on my tongue, letting me kiss her deeply. I ground myself against her roughly then drew back, breathing hard.

"I'm sorry," I murmured. "I got carried away."

She stared up at me with luminous eyes the color of the sea beneath a stormy sky. "You don't need to apologize to me," she whispered, repeating my own words from earlier back at me.

"Don't I?"

I kissed her again, finding her clothes and dressing her like a doll before I forgot my silent promise to her, laid her out and taught her every-thing I knew about pleasure and how many edges there were to the strange shape of it.

Because this girl was mine in every way and I'd be damned if I let one day with her ever be enough.

She tucked herself against me, her arms wrapped around my waist, cheek resting against my chest as she stood on trembling legs inside the circle of my arms as I directed the boat home.

The long way around.

CHAPTER FIVE

BELLA

My peace lasted as long as the walk to the door to the beach house where Falcon refused to let go, kissing me long after was probably socially acceptable, except that neither of us cared any longer. I'd only met him the night before. Already he'd broken through barriers I spent years erecting around myself in a bid to keep out creepers and stalkers...and sweet-hearts like himself that were destined to break untried hearts like mine.

He finally let me go, his eyes reflecting the claim that he didn't state in so many words but that his touch conveyed anyway. His hold tightened at the last minute as he reeled me back into his chest. "Tonight. Tomorrow. I need to see you again."

I laughed and batted at him, but it wasn't like I was trying that hard to extricate myself from his embrace. "I need to sleep. *You* need to sleep." I pushed at his shoulder when he kissed along my throat and sighed, too blissed out to really care.

"I'll live without sleep. Or we can find a place to snooze together. Picnic?" He raised his head and waggled his eyebrows.

"Deal." I grinned as his eyes lit up. "You're insatiable. In a few days. *After* you have slept. Promise." I kissed him lightly and let myself into the house while he was still professing undying love of some random description at the base of top flight of the beach house stairs.

I hoped he didn't trip over himself and tumble several flights as he walked backwards, still waving to me like a lovelorn.

Aren't we?

And cue worry. That's all it took for my anxiety to spike. I watched him cross the road and head away from the house, down the hill and back to the marina. Actually, my preference would have been to watch him walk all the way to the marina where he would have been the size of an ant in the end from my point of view, but a voice from the back of their house pulled my attention away from his spectacular frame.

"Dad?" I called, wandering through the level I was on.

I placed Falcon's hoodie that he still wouldn't let me return on the marble benchtop in the kitchen. I checked the study, but that was empty too, through the desk was messy, like he had been working in there earlier. "Where are you?"

It took me a flight up the stairs to the bedrooms, then down a different flight of stairs into the living area below and out the back to the ground level garage below to find him standing in a darkened corner, tapping away at his phone.

"Dad? What are you doing all the way down here?" As far as I knew, he had never touched the tool chests or any of the mechanical equipment that came with the house, gifted on from the previous owner who didn't want to take anything with them.

He mumbled something, and as I inched closer, I noted the half empty bottle of liquor with a label I couldn't make out in the dim light standing by his side.

"Are you okay?" I reached for the bottle and slid it off the workbench, placing it on the level below and behind something, not taking my eyes off him. "Why don't you come upstairs? I just got home. I'll make something for dinner." Guilt assuaged me for staying out so late and having fun with Falcon when Dad was home, drinking away his grief on his own.

"Dinner?" He peered at me from squinted, watery eyes. "Is it that late?"

"Yep." I took his arm, slipped his phone into my pocket when he didn't protest, and steered him up the stairs. "Come on. One at a time. What would you like to eat?"

"I was looking at photos of your mother. I miss her." His voice cracked as he hugged me, one armed.

Which would have been sweet, but he was drunk, twice my size, and we were on the stairs and it wasn't working out well. At all.

"Okay, this is good. Let's keep on moving." After a day on the water and what Falcon did with his tongue—my God, could that man kiss and...other things...I struggled to stand, let alone manage my father's weight.

We made it to the second story without side effects—like death—by some utter miracle. I parked him on the sofa, pulled off his shoes and threw some sports channels on without checking what was playing. If he didn't like it, he could fix it. But I doubted he was paying much attention at this point, either.

"She had blonde hair. Just like yours." He patted me lightly, though his attention waned.

My heart panged in my chest. "I know, Dad."

He'd taken all her photos down after we lost her, saying it hurt too much to see her. I wondered now what he felt every time he looked at me.

My steps took me too fast into the kitchen. My hip collided with the corner of the marble bench top where I'd left Falcon's jacket. I hissed breath through my teeth at the shot of pain that tore through me, rubbing my hand over the spot that would be sure to bruise. I always marked up fast. As a kid I'd been covered in spots Mom used to be certain was dirt until it wouldn't wash off. I laughed softly at the memory as I opened and closed cupboard doors with no actual plan in mind.

This is not working out so well.

"What do you want me to make for dinner?" I limped back into the upstairs living area to find Dad's head slumped over one shoulder.

He snored fairly efficiently, so I figured he wasn't going to suffocate. Sighing, I propped him up with pillows, grabbed a tub of blackberries from the fridge, and headed out the back to the wrap around verandah. A short flight of stairs took me to the rooftop where I curled on the terrace, staring out at the flickering lights of Love Beach.

At one end of the town all the buildings were clustered about—the shopping area and tourist traps, plus the bigger resorts and even a nightclub or two. Then there was the large marina right in front of that and the boardwalk that wound through everything like an endless snake.

But if I traced that same board walk all the way along, it led to the cliff tops to my left, much farther away from the town itself. A smaller bay with a tiny marina and longer jetty sparkled with the lights of the boats moored there, the few occupants who were still awake at this hour.

I grimaced belatedly, realizing how long I'd left my father alone for, knowing he didn't cope well on his own after dark. Especially here, in a place where he and Mom had been so close in the years during her supposed remission and the treatments that came afterward.

The tears that threatened in the house brewed and fell without any prior warning or shot of pain to wash them away. I dug my fingers into my palms, and when that didn't work, I stabbed my nails into my ankles.

But the grief refused to stop and poured out of me until my tears covered the backs of my hands. I hung my head, letting my hair blow around in a knotty mess as the night wind picked up as it often did here, the edge of Spring's cold kiss numbing my skin after a while.

Or maybe that was the pain I refused to accept.

My father wasn't the only one with grief issues.

It took my phone several beeps to tell me I had incoming messages.

"Sorry," I muttered my apology out of pure habit to the inanimate object as I checked the unknown number, straining through my blurred vision to read the texts.

> UNKNOWN: I enjoyed today.
>
> UNKNOWN: Be able to sleep better if I knew I could see you tomorrow.
>
> UNKNOWN: Make it a date, my Bella.

I swallowed hard. *My Bella.* My thumb fumbled the keypad in my haste to reply as I saved his name in my phone.

BELLA: You really are crazy. I didn't
give you this number.

FALCON: Perks of the crazy that's
me, I guess.

BELLA: Keep your crazy over there.

BELLA: But thank you for today.

FALCON: You're welcome. I
enjoyed myself. 😝

BELLA: 😊

FALCON: I know you enjoyed what
we did. You can say it.

BELLA: I did. Thank you.

FALCON: I heard you whisper that.
I'll see you tomorrow.

BELLA: Maybe 💟

I closed my phone, and stared out at the dark water.
The tiny lights on the very much not tiny boat where
I knew Falcon would be tonight — sleeping or other-
wise — beckoned me.

Tomorrow.

His request seemed less like that and more
demanding, presumptuous even. But part of me
wanted to see him again, too. Maybe a little too

much. Was there such a thing? I didn't know. I was so far beyond the shoals that I couldn't see the shoreline.

I'd stayed away from relationships when I saw how much it hurt watching Dad lose Mom over the year that just extended into more years. And how much it hurt me. Maybe that was selfish, but I never wanted to experience that sort of pain that crippled him each night, made him revert to childlike thinking for most of the day while he attempted to appear normal and carry on his business efforts.

It didn't take a genius to know our finances were suffering. I just needed to finish college, get a job and then maybe somehow I would be able to support him for a change and be useful.

I kept staring at the marina for long enough to realize my eyes were dry, and that the tears had stopped. As embarrassing as the conversation with Falcon had been, the heat he drew up from low in my belly at the memory of what we did together on the boat—

He also stopped the tears for one night.

CHAPTER SIX

FALCON

Sleep evaded me as I stared at the white cabin ceiling to my private berth. The large bed usually didn't bother me, but tonight it was too large.

Too empty.

I flipped my phone over in my hand, but it was too late to call her after our brief text message conversation, well past midnight. Bella was likely asleep by now, and waking her up did neither of us any favors. Shoving my phone aside, I resisted the temptation to call her just to hear her voice again.

Christ, she'd felt so good, wrapped up in my arms late in the afternoon as we made our way back to the small town. I'd taken the long way back and it was well after nightfall by the time I motored our borrowed sailing yacht in under lights to its regular berth, texting the owner that his boat had been returned in good condition.

Then I spent the next half an hour kissing Bella and not letting her go anywhere. She'd fast become my current fixation, and I knew those were long term cravings. Once something got into my blood I couldn't just fuck it around, and fuck it out again.

Christ, just the thought of kissing her soft, warm lips, and I was hard again. Let alone how hot and wet she'd been when I stroked my fingers through her folds. I shoved my pajama pants down, fisting my cock roughly. I'd been so gentle with Bella—*mostly*—and focused on making sure she got the pleasure she needed that my own hadn't even made the list.

I spat in my palm, jerking myself hard to the memory of her moans. How fast she'd come when I told her I wanted to taste her. The way her hot little pussy contracted at the thought of denying her, and I hadn't even had my finger buried inside her. The girl had some kinks, and she didn't have a fucking clue.

I did, though. If praise and denial were on the list, we could play that game over and over until she was dripping at my feet. Filthy words and humiliation were up there, too. But first, I wanted to sink myself balls deep in her tight, wet heat, and feel her spasm around me as I kissed her and stifled all her beautiful sounds—

I bit back a deep groan of my own as ropes of warm cum decorated the back of my fist. I worked my cock slowly, eking out every last inch of pleasure at the thought of making love to the girl who tainted my every waking thought with her innocence.

"Fuck," I whispered to the darkness, thumbing the head of my cock. The overstimulation hurt, almost, but it felt good at the same time.

Minutes later I was hard again, the fantasy of her begging me on repeat as I replayed the feel of her pulsing against my hand trapped against her hot skin. I used my own cum as lubricant, working myself faster and rougher, ripping my next orgasm from me. My shout wasn't half as quiet this time.

I pushed up on shaking knees to grab a towel, wiping myself off and washed up in the small ensuite that accompanied my berth.

A quick knock at my door left me on edge.

"Yeah?" I called, towel in hand, not bothering to open it.

There was no one I wanted to see tonight, unless it was Bella. And right now all I would do with her would be to wrap her in my arms tight and pass the fuck out.

"Do you want company in there? You sounded like you could do with some." The feminine voice on the other side of the door belonged to Oliva, the girl my father and his man shared a few nights before.

Who I had shared the week prior.

Now, I wanted nothing to do with her. Only one woman occupied my mind, and she wasn't on the boat, thank Christ.

"No thanks," I said shortly.

"Are you sure?" She still hadn't left the space outside my door. "I'll make it worth your while."

I laughed, a hollow, empty sound. "Nothing you could do right now will make anything worth it. Go back to my father and beg for scraps." My words were cruel and callous, but it was the language she understood, if she didn't get the message the first time around.

I was done with the bullshit culture my father surrounded himself with. If he wanted me in his business as he constantly claimed, then we would make changes. Not a huge amount, but some.

She would be the first thing to go. He could find another whore. One who I hadn't fucked, and had no intention of touching. Ever.

My phone buzzed. I leaned across the pasha bed and grabbed for it before it slid off the other side.

DEX: My Saturday night involved a split lip and cracked ribs. How was yours?

FALCON: Licked the best pussy I've had in years. You in hospital?

DEX: Brag brag, fucker. Was there. Walked home.

FALCON: Refreshing. Zinzi patch you up?

DEX: She still doesn't know.

FALCON: That you fight? Are you fucking kidding yourself? Course she knows.

DEX: Probably. Anything goes where that girl is concerned.

FALCON: Know the feeling, brother. You need anything?

DEX: Gonna borrow your pillow. Cry on it for a while. You know.

FALCON: Whatever gets you off, man. You do you.

DEX: Roommates for life.

I tossed my phone aside and fell asleep still grinning my stupid, love drunk ass off because of the girl who lived at the top of the hill who I'd fallen for in a matter of days.

Pity she'd never fit in my world.

It took me three days and dozens of text messages to see Bella again. The opportunity to make the changes with my father I wanted to see came up and—

Yeah, I took them. Stupid ass me, because with spring break half over, I had limited time with my sire before I headed back to college.

Which also meant I had limited time remaining with Bella. The tradeoff was that I could talk to her— I just didn't get to hold her when I ached for her. And so my obsession grew.

"I like this side of you, Falcon." My father made all the approving noises while Bracchio and Olivia looked on, the latter grinding her hips away that never seemed to stop, the former staring daggers in my direction.

I knew the street boss had plenty to say about my current involvement, but my father asked me to take on more of his business. For all the times in my teenage years I pushed against the responsibilities he threw my way, the recent months apart gave me a different focus.

Hell, two days with Bella shifted my focus.

"I want to understand your vision, but I also have my own," I said in Italian, watching him as he smoked. "There are...cultural changes I would like to make."

He smirked. "I know you enjoy the parties. Sometimes. But they bore you, yes?"

I practiced my Italian on him, and he practiced his English with me. Our ongoing deal.

I inclined my head. "The internal...activities shift our focal point away from what is necessary. Let them blow off steam at other times. Keep the business floor for what it needs to be."

My father's eyebrows rose. "What do you think, Bracchio?" he asked without looking at his unofficial second.

"I think if he takes away the men's fun, they will revolt." A white toothed grin flashed gold and diamonds in my direction from his grill. "I think your son's lifespan will be short. My Don." He bowed his head in a modicum of respect that was neither.

My father laughed. "He does not miss words."

"Mince words," I corrected softly.

He waved a hand. "Mix. Mince. We can do either with our enemies. But we must be kind to our friends. The men may drink in the main room. The woman may stay there. Drugs, too. But if they want to fuck, they can find their own space later, yes? A medium ground." He shot me a side eye.

"Middle ground." I nodded. "It's a solid compromise. If it meets your approval, of course," I addressed Bracchio without looking at him.

Neither of us needed his approval, and my remark was laced with sarcasm. He wasn't the only one with a truncated lifespan, and now he knew it.

Wisely, the man on the other side of my father's desk with a whore on his lap did not speak.

"Good. We are in agreement. Tell the men they find a new place to fuck in, eh? I hear there's a nice club in town. Half go tonight, the other half tomorrow. Put a tab on the bar before you leave." He nodded to me.

"Before I...?" I knew my father hated repeating himself, but I wanted to be clear on his expectations.

"You've worked hard these last days. So, have your time off. Take her on a date."

"Who?"

He laughed at me. "Don't try to keep secrets from me, Falcon. It does not work well."

I smirked and rose, bowing at the waist as was our custom.

He gestured me closer. I frowned but walked around the corner of his desk, hugging him and letting him kiss my cheeks when he motioned me to bend down. "Bracchio and the slut. Get them gone before we leave this silly little town, yes?"

"Yes, father," I said formally. "I'll be back in a few days."

That's all he would give me before his job had to be done, and we left Love Beach. All the time I had remaining with Bella.

I needed to make the most of it.

CHAPTER SEVEN

BELLA

I walked through the crowds I usually avoided, winding my way between the night market stalls and headed into the traveling carnival that had set up the weekend prior. I had avoided this place at all costs, but tonight I was feeling suicidal enough to actually attempt to people.

Dad wasn't speaking to me, or anyone from what I could tell. I'd managed calls from three aunts I didn't want to deal with this week to deliver proof of life. Falcon had messaged nonstop for the first two days of his absence, saying he had work to do for his family, which I understood, and then his chatter reverted to radio silence.

Where the doubts crept in.

So rather than sit at home and stare at the world wondering what went on in it that I missed in a seriously understated case of FOMO once Dad predictably passed out, I walked down the hill. My feet took me all the way past the marina without once looking in the direction of Falcon's boat, and led me into the town.

Through all the people. The music. The smells.

I was a good halfway through the carnival when my people-phobia set in and I decided I'd had enough. Unfortunately, that meant wandering back through all those same people to get back home.

I sucked in a deep, fortifying breath determined to manage my internal chaos, and choked on the terrifying scent of burning hotdog.

"It's pretty bad."

I pivoted on my heel, my eyes streaming as I took in Falcon, dressed in a white loose fitting shirt, loose white pants and brown loafers.

He looked nothing like a mafia prince, and everything like a normal beach town holiday maker. Or the early twenty something he was on spring break from college.

"It's feral," I choked a little more, swiping the back of my hand across my eyes.

He took pity on me, though the corners of his mouth stayed fixed in that enigmatic smile as he studied my plight. After a second he relented, catching my shoulders and guiding me away from the smoke that billowed around me.

"Are you okay?" He swept my hair out of my face, twisting it into a neat bun at the back of my neck and securing it with my elastics without being asked. He tucked the flyaway ends back, stroking my cheeks with his thumbs. "I missed you," he said quietly.

I looked up at him, all the words I wanted to say from the last days not tumbling out of my mouth because they got lodged somewhere in my throat behind a swamp of doubt and self-consciousness. And an excess of carnie smoke.

"I smell like burnt hotdog," I muttered.

"Only a little. Come on." He caught my hand, leading me away from the center of the carnival to a small coffee cart set up to one side of sideshow alley. The lights still flashed too brightly, but the sounds were more muted here. "What do you want?"

"Ah–" I hadn't thought to bring my purse with me because I had no intention of doing anything but walk and clear my head, not fill it with undesirable smoke and burning things. "I'm good," I said quickly.

He bumped my hip with his. "It's a coffee, Bella. I'm not buying your family business." His eyes weren't laughing when he said that, and his gaze darkened when he looked down at me. "I like that dress."

I squeezed the soft green cotton of my maxi length peasant dress. "It's one of my favorites. Um, matcha latte? With vanilla please," I added when his eyebrows did their thing again. "You look pretty too," I whispered, leaning in.

He snorted out a laugh. "Damn, I missed you."

His arm slipped around my waist in a possessive gesture as he held out a card. Within a minute I was holding an oversized steaming hot matcha latte that slipped down my throat.

"Thank you," I whispered.

"You weren't gonna eat anything again, were you?" He tightened his hold on me. "Were you married to walking around here?"

"No. I've had enough."

"Good." He guided us back through the crowd to the boardwalk that led past the marina to the clifftop. Somehow the crowd was more manageable with him by my side. "Sorry I wasn't around much the last few days. Dad was available and... I don't get to see him much." He fell silent for a long minute. "He's still my father, even if I don't always like him."

I swallowed hard. "I know what you mean. At least yours is...functioning."

"Semi." He laughed again and pressed a kiss to the top of my head. "Are you wearing the right–" He checked down. "You are actually wearing shoes. I'm impressed. Want to check out the view from up there?" He nodded to the clifftop.

It was a steep looking walk, but thankfully there were no people on it, especially at night.

I shrugged. "I'm game."

"You've never been?" He looked at me askance as we passed the jetty. "Will you wait here for me?"

I nodded, and he took off at a run, heading back toward his boat. I found a cement pylon and planted my butt, finishing my drink by the time he loped back toward me. A bundle was under tucked one arm, and he'd slung a different gray jacket to the one I'd stolen from his across his shoulders. That, he promptly took off.

"This is for us." He nodded to the picnic rug under his arm. "This is for you." He shrugged off the jacket and wrapped it around my shoulders.

"I'm getting a collection."

"Good." His gaze darkened as he looked at me, a

shadow flittered behind his eyes. Something unspoken passed there, but after a moment he grabbed my hand, finishing his drink and binned both of our cups. "Captain said it's a bit of a walk, but worth it. Do you need to be back any time soon?" He tacked that last bit on casually.

I shook my head. Dad had passed out later than usual, which meant he would also wake up later. "No, why?"

"Because Cap also said the sunrise is stunning." Falcon reached out to brush his thumb across my bottom lip. "Are you up for that?"

I didn't answer him because I couldn't, so I nodded instead. He seemed to understand, dipping his head to brush his mouth lightly over mine. Just once. That's all.

My heart pitter-pattered away in my chest as his hand closed firmly around mine. We walked in silence, taking the steep walk slow, enjoying the night's quiet air.

We reached the top without too much panting or disgracing ourselves. His hand never left mine, and he never towed me up the hill or walked ahead of me, just keeping pace.

Whatever or whoever Falcon Gianio was behind

closed doors with his family, he was a different man with me.

Low undergrowth opened out to a small expanse of rock and grass. A few beer bottles littered the far side of the clearing, but it was cleaner where Falcon laid out the picnic rug, planting his ass in the middle with his legs set out in a vee shape. He crooked one finger at me where I huddled in his jacket back against the shrubbery, neither of us breaking our unspoken vow of silence.

The cliff face was sheer, maybe a dozen feet away from where he laid out the rug on the ground. Beyond that the sea looked black, except for a single shimmering triangle where the moon's light reflected on the dark water.

He leaned back and caught my hand as I stared toward a horizon I could no longer see, tugging me down to the space between his legs. Warm arms wrapped around me as he rested his chin on my head.

I sank into him with a sigh. "I thought this was going to be scary."

Falcon stiffened. "What was going to be scary?" He kept his tone light as he traced patterns on my collarbone, sliding his hands inside the jacket he leant me.

I have to give this one back. I cannot keep it.

I swallowed at the thought of parting ways with him when he left. I knew this couldn't be forever. A silly notion; we were a spring break fling at best, something fun to be enjoyed in the moment and here I was, adding drama to it.

"Nothing." I brushed the thought away. "Tell me how everything went with your Dad?"

He laughed in my ear. "Tell me what was going to be so scary about being alone with me," he murmured, brushing his lips across my temple, then my cheek.

I swallowed, knowing he would feel my nerves, read them as I did his. "I shouldn't have said anything—" I started.

"Be honest with me. Remember, Bella? Have you forgotten already?" he murmured. He tugged me back into him when I pulled away, and I let him, closing my eyes to shut out the world, noise from the day intruding on the peace of the night with him.

I knew what he expected me to say but...that wasn't what terrified me. Well, not entirely.

"I'm scared of the night passing so fast that when I open my eyes, you're gone again," I whispered my confession in a rushed breath.

The wind caught it, whisking my words away so

fast I wondered that I'd said anything at all. Falcon stilled at my back for a breath. His hands flexed on my skin before he cupped my chin and tilted my head back, though he didn't kiss me, not entirely. Not yet.

"Christ, I thought you were worried about me hurting you. That I wouldn't stop if you told me that's not what you wanted—" His breath hitched and I tipped my head upward, pressing up to find my mouth with his.

"That's not it. Well, a tiny bit, but what girl isn't scared of that with someone new? That's...it's a thing. But what I'm scared of is it disappearing. This. Us. All of what I feel going by too fast that I miss it even when I'm here, with you."

CHAPTER EIGHT

BELLA

"*Christ.*" His mouth crashed down over mine in a hard kiss that he softened almost immediately. "I'm sorry. I don't want to be rough with you." He drew back, his eyes begging an apology.

"Stop," I murmured, and he reared back, though he still held me, his hands tangled in my hair. "Not like that. Stop worrying, Falcon. I'm not going anywhere unless you push me away."

"Not happening." He lowered his mouth to mine again, slower this time, and kissed me gently.

I wasn't sure who moaned first. Our sounds mingled in the night air as he traced the shape of my lips with his tongue. The same as on the boat, Falcon never rushed me, or us. Everything movement was slow and sweet as he slipped his tongue onto my mouth. One hand closed delicately around my throat, tilting my head back to him. The other skated along my front, gathering the material of my dress in his fist.

Minutes into our broken kisses his breath came in hard pants. "This is more difficult than I expected," he muttered.

"Then stop trying to control everything." I rolled my shoulders back, arching into his touch when he brushed his thumb beneath my breast. I let out a gasp. "I like that."

"Yeah?" His breath came heavy against my lips and then he was kissing me again, a little faster, but not rough. Whatever he'd decided, he kept a tight rein on his control, only letting out as much as he wanted to give in this moment.

"Mmm." I made a non-committal noise until he used all his fingertips to stroke my breast. Sensation tingled over me, and I writhed in my place between his legs. "Falcon–"

"Fuck," he growled, hauling me against him.

Our limbs tangled, as he shoved the jacket off me, tossing it aside and shifted, scooping me tight against his body. My back pressed against the mat, and suddenly I was looking up at him where he lay between my legs, every inch of him arched over. And every inch was suddenly very apparent.

"You know how I said I wasn't afraid of that, much?" I bit my lip.

He leaned down and tugged my lip free with his teeth, licking and sucking on the tingling flesh until I whimpered and twisted beneath him.

"Keep moving like that and you'll have nothing at all to be afraid of," he promised me in a low voice.

"Oh," was the only sound that came out of my mouth as I stared into unforgiving eyes that bore into me.

"But you tell me to stop and I'll do it," he promised, stroking his knuckles along my ribs, and over my hip. The material of my dress drew tight across my belly as he flexed his hand. "Be very damn clear about what you want or don't want tonight, Bella. Because I know exactly who I want, and it's you."

"I—" My brain stalled. My mouth too.

The corner of his quirked. He kissed me gently. "It's okay, beautiful. Am I scaring you yet?"

"It gets worse?"

I sighed when he didn't answer, kissing me deeply until all of my panicked thoughts filtered away. He pulled back to brace one arm above me and flicked the top button undone on his shirt then pulled it over his head.

He was covered in ink, muscle, and completely waxed.

And the ink covered a smattering of scars that were scarier than anything we would do tonight.

"Touch me, Bella." His voice tautened as he toyed with the strap of my dress. "I want this off you."

Holding my breath because breathing no longer seemed logical, I stroked my hands along his chest, over defined pecs and planes of muscle that flexed beneath my fingers. Apparently I wasn't the only one holding my breath. I found the long, pale slice that wound its way across his shoulder, traced that to a group of three tiny dots situated much lower that the ink I thought was a raven in flight didn't quite cover.

"Are these...?"

"One of my father's not-friends decided to take a few shots at him. I was in the road." He shrugged like taking three bullets to his side was nothing.

"You were *in the road?*" My voice rose a little on that last. "What, by design? By accident? How—"

He caught my hand, kissing my fingers and

tucked it into his over my head. "I stepped in, Bella. I didn't want to lose another parent."

I stared. "How old were you?" I whispered, my heart pounding.

"Eighteen."

Three years ago. The year his mother died, from what he'd told me earlier. When I'd lost mine. I closed my eyes, my heart rate accelerating. "Falcon, I can't—"

He covered his mouth with mine, breathing into me. I sucked in his breath by reflex, my eyes flaring wide as he drew back.

"Breathe, Bella," he whispered. "I'm alright. We're here. Just here. Now. It's just us."

His hand fisted my dress and pulled it up at one side, flicking his thumb under my panties beneath.

"Tell me to stop, Bella," he murmured. "Tell me no."

I met his eyes that searched my face as he pressed his erection into me. His heart pounded so fast and hard I could hear it. This wasn't his first time by far. Without asking, I knew that much about him. But this moment seemed to matter as much to him as it did to me.

I could have stammered and stuttered through some explanation to him, but instead I lifted my head and pressed my mouth to his, parting my lips and slid my tongue into his mouth.

His groan set every nerve ending in me on fire as he squeezed my hand tight in his and ground into me. The hand hooked into my panties tugged downward as he lifted his weight off me for a moment. I helped him pull them free of my body.

"I want to see all of you." He swallowed hard. "But I understand if you aren't okay with that." The admission looked like it hurt him to say.

"I want to see you too," I blurted.

His smile eased the pressure building inside me. "Anything, for you." He kissed me as he flicked the straps on my shoulders, baring the tops of my breasts.

His lips touched every exposed inch as he worked on his belt and pushed his pants down. Somewhere along the line he kicked his shoes off. Mine came off too as he peppered kisses over my skin, peeling the dress from my body, licking and sucking as he traveled his way lower. Falcon nipped the soft skin at my belly lightly, and froze with his hand on my hip.

"What happened here?" His voice turned all rough and growly as he pressed his thumb down on tender flesh.

"Huh? Oh, I ran into the kitchen bench. I bruise up pretty fast." I laughed, shrugging it off.

"No one hurt you?" He looked up my body at me.

"Just me." I snorted. "Because I'm so graceful."

"You are," —he kissed my hip, then my stomach — "so beautiful. Nothing and no one," —he licked my inner thigh, spreading my legs apart with the heels of his hands— "will ever compare to you."

"So poetic," I muttered, then gasped when he licked my thigh so close to my sensitive skin. "Oh, wow, don't do— fuck," I whispered when he bit down.

"You need to swear more," he murmured, and bit on my other side.

"Keep doing that and I will— ow," I cried. "Stop that!" I slapped at the top of his head lightly. "Why are you biting me?"

"You said your skin bruises easily." He shrugged like that made it all that much clearer.

"And?" I frowned at him. "I thought you liked me. Don't, you know, eat me." my cheeks heated at the memory of him doing exactly that.

"A bit more than like, beautiful." He pushed his body along mine and kissed me hard, possessively.

"If you have marks on you, they sure as fuck better be *my* damn marks."

"Oh." Comprehension settled in at the same time as the weight of him pressed between my thighs. "Falcon—"

"Easy, Bella. Not just yet." He slid one hand between us, rubbing his fingers over my pussy, exploring and groaning. "Fuck, you feel so soft and damn good. I can't wait to slide into you. You know this will hurt, right?"

I glared at him. "Virgin. Not idiot."

"Noted." He grinned and flicked my clit.

My sass transformed to molten heat. "I can't—" I writhed beneath him as he taught me things I didn't know about my body, what I needed, how I needed him to touch me.

"You will. Again and again," he promised me as he flicked my clit again and the world darkened.

My throat turned raw on a scream I didn't remember voicing when he kissed me next, though his finger pressed deep inside me, working slowly. My body stretched and ached around him in a sensory overload I struggled to process.

"Again," he whispered, working his hand faster.

I tightened around the intrusion, my cries muffled by his deep kisses as he brought me to the edge of insanity again and again. My fingernails dug into his arms until I was sure I'd leave my own fresh set of scars on his body.

"Too much," I gasped as bliss broke over me again like the waves lapping at the base of the cliff face below us.

"Is there such a thing?" he teased, echoing my thoughts, and withdrew his hand gently, playing with me still. "Do you want me to stop?"

I knew what he was asking, and I shook my head. "Please don't let me go. Not tonight."

"Never will." He kissed me again, sealing his vow between our lips as he pushed my hand between us, closing my fingers around him. "Touch me, Bella," he murmured. Begged, almost.

I traced the shape of him, my panic growing as I knew this would hurt but the way his breath hissed between his teeth when I touched him pushed those thoughts aside. I watched his eyes, curious at his reactions as I rubbed my thumb over his velvety head, and closed my hand gently around him. His fist covered mine, squeezing hard. I let out a super unsexy squeak.

"Did I hurt you?"

He laughed. "No, but if you keep touching me that lightly like that I won't last more than a minute.

Squeeze. Like this." He pumped our hands together until his head dropped to watch us work his cock between our hands before he pushed my hand away on shuddering breath and kissed me. "Too good, Bella. Christ, I want to last for you."

"I wanted to taste you," I said shyly.

"Next time," he promised, stretching one hand gently over my head and folding our fingers together. "Is this okay?"

I nodded, biting my lip. "Yes. Please," I whispered.

"Good girl." He nodded and inched forward, halting suddenly. "Christ, I'm a fool. I'm not thinking straight tonight." He reached for his jeans, but I stopped him.

"I'm on the shot. It helps with, um... you know..." Hell, could I be more embarrassing? Here the man above me was basically a mafia princeling sex god, and I was stuttering all over him.

"It helps with cramps?" he asked kindly, squeezing out hands together. "I get it, Bella. Mom was very open with me, tried to prep me for one day looking after someone I cared about." He swallowed hard, staring down at me.

"I—" And we were back to stuttering land.

"It's okay," he said softly. "I'm going to go slow. Tell me when it's too much, okay?"

I just nodded, running dry of anything useful to say.

He leaned down and kissed me, cupping my breast in one hand and stroking the nipple until I ached and arched beneath him. Heat pooled between my legs and he moaned too, pushing against my entrance. The head of him stretched me and I gasped.

"Hurting you?" he asked, stilling.

"It's a lot," I managed.

"You're tight as hell," he agreed. "Can I touch you?"

I nodded as he tucked me into his shoulder and slid his hand between us, working my clit gently. I moaned, already over-stimulated as he pushed his way inside me, stalling when he pressed against me and my entrance ached around his size. Was he big? I had no frame of reference. My mind tangented, and his hand stilled, then pinched me lightly until I gasped.

"Bella, look at me," he commanded softly. "This next part is going to hurt. I can't stop that. But I can show your body pleasure afterward. Alright?"

"Please, just—"

He surged forward, filling me with his hard length. My world turned white, blinding me. I opened my mouth on a silent scream as he swore above me. Faintly, I became aware of him cradling my head in one hand, his weight still balanced over me. But the pain that ripped through me was all encompassing. I couldn't get a breath in, let alone feel anything.

"Shhh, Bella. You're okay. Christ, I'm so fucking sorry." Falcon kissed the corner of my lips. "Jesus, girl. Be okay for me." His worried eyes swam into view as I blinked for him.

"Fuck," I whispered softly, not in a good way, once I could speak again. "That really—"

"Hurts." Falcon nodded. "I promised I'd remind your body how to feel pleasure. Let me."

He kissed me again, light touches of lips and tongue that reminded me to breathe as I sank into his arms, and clung to him. His thumb brushed across my clit, strumming gently in the excess fluid spread over my flesh from our excess playtime before.

If I'd thought the orgasms he gave me before were amazing, it had nothing on this. For the first time I came around the solid feeling of him lodged deep inside me, lying completely still. His moan echoed mine as I unraveled around him, clamping down hard on his length as I cried his name to the darkened sky.

"Jesus," he swore, jerking his hips. "You are a new form of torture, Bella. Fuck—" He swallowed hard, and gripped my hip. "I promised you it would be slow, didn't I?"

"You promised you wouldn't leave or let me go."

"I can do that."

He began to move, slow at first, his arm wound around me, his other hand clasped tight to mine holding us linked together. One hand slipped down to throw my leg over his thigh as he drove his hips deeper.

"Falcon—" I cried out, arching as he growled above me.

"Christ, you're the most beautiful creature," he rasped as I fell apart for him again, trembling.

My entire body shook as he roared his own need and slammed into me three times, seating himself deep. I could *feel* him pulsing inside me as he came, pressing his weight down on me.

And I'd never felt so not alone in this place where I'd been so lonely without him.

CHAPTER NINE

FALCON

The sun rose over us as Bella slept on my chest. We missed the sunrise together, but the weight of her curled against me beneath my jacket may have been one of the best damn experiences of my life.

Topped only by the pure, unadulterated trust she gave me last night when she let me take something from her I still wasn't sure she should have let me have.

She stirred as I stroked her hair, tangling my fingers in the silky strands and untangling them just to amuse myself, because I could. She'd put her dress back on afterward and I'd covered her in my jacket, pressing us together on the rug for warmth, but the wind had dropped. I ached to sleep with her naked, just to feel her pressed to me skin to skin.

Wake up with her in the sunshine, roll her over and kiss her until she moaned for me.

But I didn't want to hurt her or wake her early this morning, so I simply stroked her hair and held her tight.

Like she asked.

She'd also asked that I didn't leave her. That seemed an impossibility, but I had an idea on that front, though I wasn't sure how she'd take the offer when I made it.

"Morning, Falcon." She looked up at me, all heavy eyes, dozy with sleep.

So fucking beautiful.

I don't deserve her.

"Morning, beautiful. How did you sleep?"

"Good." She pressed into me with a contented sigh.

I swore my heart would explode with every fresh sound she made. "Hurting?"

She shrugged. "A bit. In the right way, though."

I swallowed. "Yeah."

Fuck, she was brave. I saw how much taking me hurt her last night, but she did it anyway. The feel of her clamping down on me afterward tested every inch of my resolve. I continued stroking her hair, and rested my head back on the rug. Sure, my back ached a bit but I'd survive. She felt too damn good where she was to move.

"Shouldn't we—"

"Nope." I pressed my hand to the back of her head and held her to my chest. "If you get up, I'll find out just how many swats it takes to mark up that pretty, pale backside of yours."

"You promise?"

I raised my head. "Girl, I don't know if you just sassed me or bratted out on me, but damn if I don't want to find out." I squeezed her tight. "Don't. You. Move."

"Yes, Falcon." She settled into me, her weight heavier with every breath that left her body, tension releasing from her slim frame.

So fucking perfect right where she was. The natural submissive in her called to me, but it was the spirit in her that sassed me when she needed to that I loved the most.

Loved.

I swallowed hard and shoved a hand through my hair. *Fuck Me.* My breaths came short. But the panic I expected didn't slam into me with the force it should have.

Eventually, my existential crisis abated and the sun flared into my eyes. And my bladder decided it couldn't take any more. "I'll be back in a minute. Alright?" I pulled her up my body and kissed her puffy lips.

Christ, she did mark up fast. Her lips were red and swollen and I hadn't even been that rough with her. We could have some fun with that later. I stroked her cheek as her lashes fluttered and she gave me a dozy nod, snuggling back beneath the jacket when I slipped out from beneath her.

By the time I found a tree to relieve myself against and returned, Bella was sitting upright, her hair unwound as she ran her hands through the long strands, pulling out the knots.

"I can do that for you," I offered, coiling some of the flyaway waves in my fingers.

She bit her lip, then nodded. I knew that look. Pressing a kiss to her temple, I worked out the knots gently with my fingers and began a long braid down her back as I sought out the right words. "No one has looked after you for a long time, have they?"

She jerked like I had pinched her. "That's– Dad just needs a lot of help," she rushed to explain, twisting on the spot. "He hasn't been the same since—"

I pressed my fingers over her lips. "I know you love him, beautiful. You don't need to explain that to me. I have an...easily influenced father of my own."

I didn't want to portray him as weak, not even to a girl who I suspected would understand him just fine. Even if she probably wouldn't like him or any of his habits. Hell, I hated him half the time myself, even if I'd still step in front of him the next time someone tried to end his life.

If I was there that day.

That she mightn't be able to deal with the lifestyle that came with my family deep stung at chest level. I tied her hair off at the end and dropped the braid over her shoulder. "Can I walk you back home?"

I still had a few more days before we hit a critical level where I'd have to walk away from her, but the job my father set earlier hung over me. I needed to get that done so I could work out how to keep Bella near me, if that was what she wanted.

I cleared my throat when she didn't move or say anything. "I know we just met, but I wondered if—"

"Yes."

She didn't stutter this time, didn't stumble over her words or misspeak.

The corner of my mouth crooked up. "You haven't heard the offer yet."

Bella twisted, seeking out my hand with hers. I laced our fingers together as she turned to me on her knees. "Is it something that means we aren't a state away from college? Because I looked Rippton U up the other day. It's in Cali. That... is not where I go to school."

I smirked. "Smart girl." I tugged her closer, sliding my hands to her waist when she crept toward me on her hands and knees. Hell, the view of her like that in her soft green dress did things to my head that I didn't question right now.

"Maybe." Her smile faded. "It's an exclusive school. My father's business... he isn't good at paying attention. Not since..." She looked down at the rug, studying our entwined hands. "I haven't checked recently but I think we're as close to broke as we can be without selling everything up."

"Ah." I leaned in. "I'm pretty sure Rippton offers scholarships." *Or I'll make my own if she won't let me pay her tithe.* The school demanded the students pay their personal fees out of their own pocket directly. But that system could easily be overturned. Money did that. "We can work something out. They have an excellent art department. I'm sure there's something you could enroll in that would suit." The edge of desperation settled into my words.

"Maybe," she whispered.

I kissed her, needing her closer. "Try this with me," I begged, not caring how I sounded. "I know it's been a few days. I know this is crazy, but—"

Christ, her stutter was contagious. The whole thing was laughable. I should head back to the marina, do what my father required of, and sail the fuck away.

I knew I wouldn't.

"I want to try." She pressed her body to mine. "It's weird and I know I'm not supposed to latch onto the first person who—" A small frown interrupted her smooth skin when she didn't complete her sentence.

"Don't you dare finish that," I threatened lightly after it became clear she wouldn't anyway. "Whichever asshole gave you that idea is an idiot. Give your respect and love to whoever makes you feel the safest and happiest, Bella. Make it your choice, not the end result of some system that was never designed with you in mind."

She blinked at me. "That was quite a speech."

I smirked. "Been known to happen." I shoved up to my knees and kissed her again, then stood. "I've got one job to do, then I'm yours. I'll walk you to the jetty if you won't let me take you all the way home?"

She nodded, letting me haul her upright. We stood there, latched together, wobbling and giggling together like the teens we weren't. Her kisses left me heady and I knew I wouldn't forget this woman fast as she left me at the end of the jetty with a soft kiss that sliced through my heart and the sort of goodbye I never wanted to hear again.

Because she made it sound like she meant it for the last time.

Everything we'd talked about slammed into me as I gripped her waist tight when she turned away.

"No." My voice came out too loud and clear for a still morning, the sound sure to carry over the water. "You do not leave me like this, Bella. Not now, or ever. That sounded like—" I ground my teeth together, boring my gaze into hers.

"Goodbye," she whispered.

"Do you believe that?" I caught her chin and tipped her head back.

She shook her head, then shrugged. "I don't know what to believe. You're so perfect and beautiful and sweet. And I'm just..." She shrugged again.

I pulled her against my chest, the need to claim her consuming me. "I need you to listen to me,

Bella," I said in a low voice, but loud enough for her to hear me clearly. "Some time since I met you I'd fallen in love with you and no amount of pretending that hasn't happened will change that. Shh," I added when she opened her mouth. "Please, hear me out. I'm shit at this stuff, so please, let me say this. Last night—that nearly broke me. Seeing you hurting because I did that to you? Fuck, Bella. That was one of the hardest things I've ever done. But one of the most beautiful, too. Because you came to me, willingly. Me, of all people. I'm so far from fucking perfect it's not funny. I'm not some good boy you take home to daddy, beautiful. You do know what it is I do, don't you?" I raised both eyebrows.

She huffed and tapped at my face. "Stop that. You'll give yourself a headache."

"Bella," I warned, though a reluctant laugh bubbled up inside me.

"Yes, I know what you do, Falcon," she said crossly. "I'd have to be a fool to not know you're mafia. You were shot, for heaven's sake. I'm sure you do your fair share of that too."

I blinked at her. "Do you understand the connotations of that? Because most people run screaming at this point if they aren't in the life."

Her head tipped to one side as she watched me

with that sweetly curious expression. "Are you going to shoot me?"

"No, Bella."

"Are you going to hurt me?"

"No." I squeezed her waist until she made a different sort of sound. I growled low in response. "But I might show you other things I like."

"Good. Then I want to learn how to give you as much pleasure as you gave me last night. And I want to understand all the ink on you. Plus probably a thousand other questions that will annoy the hell out of you."

"Too cute."

"Okay, so are we good then?" She smiled brightly at me.

I blinked. "I still can't work out if it's sass or brat but damn girl, we are going to talk about that spanking I promised you." I dropped a hand to her ass and squeezed hard until she whimpered deliciously. My lips brushed her ear. "And your thighs do bruise well. I checked while you slept."

Her hitched breath did strange things to my cock.

"You checked—"

She could think on that one for a while.

"Go home, Bella. I'll message when I'm done,

alright?" I kissed her deeply, then decided to hell with all of it, twisting her hair in my fist and made it a touch rougher. My tongue drove into her mouth as her finger closed into fists on my shirt.

When I drew back, she gasped for breath and her cheeks were stained the prettiest pink.

"Is that how you usually kiss?" she asked faintly.

"I told you who I am, Bella. I'll be sweet with you as long as you need. But I like to play rough now and then."

Her nails dug into my pecs. "Show me?"

"Fuck, you are a little brat." What sort of monster had I unleashed with her? And I still wasn't convinced that she didn't love every damn minute of what we did. "Go home, Bella," I ordered. My tone softened, along with my kisses. "I'll see you soon. Then we can talk about something more...permanent, if that's what you want."

She nodded and walked away when I let her go, glancing over her shoulder once. I waited until she disappeared around the corner at the top of the hill, then I made my way back to the boat.

This time, we hadn't said goodbye at all.

CHAPTER TEN

BELLA

Falcon left his wallet in his jacket. The second one I stole—by accident. By the time I realized, I was back home and he had returned to his boat. I sent through a few messages, but he didn't answer. I remembered he said he had work to do, and I knew he'd be busy but I figured he might need the wallet, so I walked back down the hill after checking my own father was still asleep—snoring after last night's bender, thankfully.

The sun had risen high by the time I reached the jetty, and my body hurt kind of all over just as I had confessed to Falcon earlier. Still, I walked slowly along the jetty, marking out the smaller yacht that still looked big to me that we had taken out the week before. A man with sandy blond hair worked in it. I gave him a wave as he passed and he murmured a quiet *good morning* that I returned.

The closer I got to Falcon's boat, the more misgivings I had. He'd said he would message me when he was done, and I hadn't heard back yet. I was on the cusp of turning around and heading back home when a feminine voice hailed me from the level above the water line. I looked up—right up a very short dress that appeared to cover a bikini that wasn't really doing its job.

"Hi," the blond girl called out, waving enthusiastically. "Are you Falcon's girlfriend?"

"Uh–" Was I? We hadn't really talked about it. "I just came to return some of his things." I held up the jacket and the concealed wallet. "I figured he might need them today. Is he about?"

"Oh, he's here somewhere." She gestured to the boat that, at a glance in the daylight, looked as big as a house moored at the end of the long jetty.

"Okay..."

"Come on." She clattered down a set of stairs in heels. I winced, thinking of the other young man and his well loved boat. "I'll show you around."

"Uh—" I had the vocal strength of a sea cucumber today. "Sure, just for a sec."

Long enough to find his room, deliver his things, and walk out again.

"This way!" The girl in the sparkly dress that looked like it was better suited to last night's cocktail party led me down a set of stairs to a living area that looked like it *hosted* last night's cocktail party, and more.

You know who he is. You know what he does.

But seeing the evidence of baggies of drugs laid out around me was a bit more than I expected to handle straight up this morning. Apparently, I had more than one cherry popped in the last twenty-four hours. The girl didn't seem to notice, though as she led me through to the other side of the room. "You take too long." She pouted.

I mean, maybe that worked on guys? Not that I'd have a clue. I looked around. "I can just leave this here, and—"

"Oh, the cleaners will be in soon. Don't leave anything that might be lost." She giggled.

I frowned. "That's one hell of a stereotype."

Her giggles stopped. "What a way to announce you're a bitch."

O-kay. "Which way is the Falcon's room, please?"

"I'm sure you can find it." She flounced off through another side door that slammed and locked —audibly—with a sharp click.

I was left standing alone in the trashed living area.

Turning in circles, I found a corridor at the other end of the room that led back the way I came just underneath it instead. Doors lined either side of the short corridor—I was sure that had another name on a boat—but none were open. I reached the second one and knocked before my nerve failed me.

"Falcon?"

Nothing. That one was locked. I tried the next, then one on the other side. It opened. I pushed it gently, poking my head inside. "Falcon—"

His head came up from where he stood unbuttoning his shirt on the other side of the bed. If he hadn't been wearing the same shirt and pants as the night we spent together, I might not have recognized him. Or the clothing.

Red that wasn't paint splattered his shirt, reaching up to stain his cheek. His hair was wild and bruising covered his jaw. Along with what might have been dirt. His sleeves were rolled to his elbows and those were covered in blood too.

Because we all knew he wasn't cosplaying.

I took a step back, but his eyes locked on me.

"Bella?" His voice rasped like gravel.

"I—"

I managed another half a step, trying to close the door that stubbornly refused to budge before it was pulled open abruptly from the inside. His hand closed around my wrist as he yanked me into his room and slammed the door shut, locking me in with him.

"What the hell are you doing here?"

I stared up at him for so long that my mouth figured out I hadn't answered him, but all my mind registered was the horror before me.

You do know what I do?

He'd been right to check in with me. Knowing and seeing were different things. The way he wore someone else's blood so casually terrified me, but worse than that I was...

Curious.

And that scared me even more.

What was wrong with me that I *wanted* to know about his life of his? I shouldn't. No normal person wanted this. And yet as he caged me in against the door with his body, his bloodied shirt hanging half open as he leaned over me, my heart raced for all the wrong reasons.

"Answer me, Bella," he softened his voice sweetly for me, and I wanted to cry.

"Don't do that," I whispered. "Don't apologize for who you are when *this* is who you are."

"You're terrified of me." His voice flattened out. "I can see it in your face."

I ignored that statement. We could work on reality later. "I came to return this." I proffered the lost jacket. "It has your wallet inside. I thought you might need it today."

He studied me and made no move to take the jacket, the only thing that made a barrier between us. His arms flexed over my head and I realized just how much muscle the man arched over me possessed.

"Who let you in?" he said finally.

"A girl. I don't know her name. Sparkly dress. Skimpy bikini. She had a bit of a temper tantrum when I called her out about being rude about the help."

He smirked. "Olivia. She can be like that. And she won't be here much longer." He raised an eyebrow significantly.

My gaze trailed down to his chest and the mess there. "Oh."

"Yeah. *Oh.* She pissed off my father. So did her boyfriend."

"Does she know?"

This is a really weird conversation. We are talking about him killing someone. Someone I just met. I think we are. Wait. Why am I okay with this?

Falcon watched me. "She's about to. Security should have stopped you before you got this far." A scream erupted at the other end of the boat. He sighed. "If I ask you to stay here, and not leave the room, will you do that? Can I trust you to stay here?"

I swallowed hard. "What happens if I leave?"

"You see things I don't want you to see." His gaze met mine and held. Unforgiving. Unyielding. "I don't want my father to ask questions I can't answer later. Not about you." He dropped a hand toward my face then pulled back and sighed. "I'm filthy. Let me get this done and I'll be back in a minute. Alright?" He watched me closely.

"Do I look like I'm about to run?"

"No." He turned us around and planted me on his oversized bed. "That's what worries me."

"Sorry," I whispered, but he was already out the door that—naturally—closed for him.

My heart ached at the absence of him, but maybe that was why I stayed. Because he'd been so sweet and I saw that side of him. Because I knew who he was and what he did from that first night, though seeing it was slightly different. I couldn't kid myself any longer. But the way he treated me spoke more about who Falcon Gianio was inside than anything he did here. No, I didn't understand his world, but I could learn it.

What I did know was that this man took his time with me, the same man who never rushed me or made me feel small or lesser than him. Who ached inside like I did. Who I had fallen head over heels for when I had no right to the night he held me in his arms and promised he'd never leave me alone.

I perched on the edge of the bed, then when he didn't come back after a while, I curled in the middle of the oversized mattress that smelled like him, and closed my eyes.

I had no idea how long I slept, only that I was exhausted beyond my limits and hadn't stopped to think about that until I finally got the chance to just sleep.

On a mafia boat in Love Beach. Not the safest place, maybe, but Falcon promised I'd be alright, and that was enough for me.

Yes, ours was a strange relationship. But he seemed to understand things about me that I barely knew about myself.

The mattress sank under his weight as he slid in beside me, wrapping me up in his arms. "You didn't leave."

I yawned. "You told me not to."

He frowned as he looked at me. "I don't understand why you aren't screaming or running."

I smiled and touched his cheek. "You look better without all the blood."

"You remember that, huh?"

"You were ages. I fell asleep." I leaned my head on his shoulder. "I think there's lots of things you need to tell me about if I stay with you, but I don't know what to ask."

He huffed his agreement. "That's a rabbit hole no one wants to fall down." He paused. "Your father came looking for you."

"Dad?" I jerked upright. "Oh, my God. I left him alone. Again. I'm a terrible daughter. Was he okay?"

Falcon did laugh this time. "No. He's far from okay, actually, but he and my father had a talk and I think we came up with a few solutions to your...problems. One is that they both understand grief, even if they deal with it in different ways. My father, who isn't a fan of telling anyone anything at all, suggested counseling."

I stared. "We have tried all this."

Falcon smirked. "It's a bit different when the Don of the mafia tells you to do something. I believe we also acquired your family business." He held up a hand when I opened my mouth with a plethora of objections at the ready. "In part. It's been gifted to me, for now. The rest is yours."

My lips twitched as I bit back my thoughts for now. "Do I want to hear the rest?"

"Brat," he muttered, kissing my temple. "There were debts. The house, not the one here. You own that outright, I believe. But the one where your father lives year round, and your school fees. The business buyout allowed for enough cash flow to cover those debts, and get the bank off your father's back. It's why he came here in the first place." Falcon groaned as he stretched, and I knew that wasn't all of it.

"Go on, tell me the rest," I sighed. "I should have known more about it all."

His knuckles grazed my jawline as he pulled me

back to rest against him. "You should have been able to rely on your father to look after you, not the other way around, Bella," he said quietly. "What I've spent the last few hours negotiating should make that easier on you both. I hope. My father is a hard man when there is something he wants on the table."

I closed my eyes. "What did he want?"

"You."

"Huh?"

"That's what your father came here to offer the night we met. Obliquely," Falcon added. "He offered the business for sale and parked you right in my path, hoping I'd see you and want you. Packaged you up all nice and pretty, like bait." He grimaced. "I remember thinking the same damn thing that night. I should have made the connection."

"I—" I stared at him. "I'm so sorry. That's so far from okay. I am—" A sickness roiled in my stomach. "Falcon, I am so sorry. I'll leave. That's— he manipulated you. Hell, that means *I* did too. I won't— we can't—"

"Whoa, girl." He caught me as I scrambled off the bed, swinging us around until we knotted together in Falcon-Bella pretzel. "Don't you run off on me. I just spent hours explaining to my father that you're my Untouchable. Don't–"

"That I'm a *what?*" A choked sort of giggle exploded from me as he broke through my panicked haze. "Sorry, but that sounds like a terrible type of gangster movie."

He smiled ruefully. "It was one, and it was cool. I'll show you sometime. I trust you. It—that scared me at first, I'll admit. But you're different. If you want me to let you go, walk away, I'll do it. But I don't want to." His expression cleared when I shook my head as he rearranged me on his lap, swinging my legs over his until I straddled him, staring him in the face. His body tensed beneath mine as he cupped my nape, his fingers massaging the muscle there. "Being Untouchable means I told my father I want you—no one else. I can't claim anyone else, Bella. I get one chance at this, and I'm claiming you. I won't let anyone hurt or touch you, especially not him." His lip curled as he dragged me closer.

Suddenly I was all too aware of my dress hiked around my thighs, the press of him as he gripped one of my hips and squeezed.

A soft, strangled sound made it out of my throat. "I don't understand."

He laughed, leaning in to press his forehead to mine. "I don't half understand why I'm doing this, either. But you're mine, Bella. In all the ways that count in my world. What probably should have been a fling just turned into something a whole lot more."

I frowned. "Is this the equivalent of proposing to me?" A huff left me. "We just met."

He studied me for a moment. "If you like."

My mouth fell open. "I— you can't do that. Falcon. I don't have to Google you to know you're wealthy as hell, especially if you just bought half of my father's business."

"I can, actually, but if you don't want me, my offer remains. It always will. My protection stands in this world, even if we aren't together. And I did buy it. Your father's business. All of it. I just reallocated shares so you got the majority instead of my father."

"Oh." my head processed that for a while and couldn't find a flaw in his logic, though I'd check everything over later. "Uh, thanks... This is overwhelming and I need time to understand it. Plus, a lawyer. My own."

"Agreed. We can do that back home."

"Home?" I stared into his dark eyes, lost yet again.

"I'm taking you back to Rippton with me. Not a word on that," he warned. "I have a crazy roommate with an even crazier fuck buddy he pines about. How much more imperfect can the world be?"

I shrugged. "Sounds perfect to me. Just find a lawyer we can both talk to—together—so I can understand everything you've just done, the contracts, and what the future looks like."

"What?" Falcon stared at me.

I leaned in, brushing my lips to the corner of his mouth. "That's usually my line," I whispered.

He swallowed. "You're coming back to Rippton with me?"

"Is that the only part you heard, Mister Mafia Prince?"

"After everything else I figured you'd fight that part."

"I want to be wherever you are," I said simply. "Especially if my father is safe and has made a weird little friend."

Falcon laughed hard and loud. "Oh fuck, Bella. I have never heard anyone describe the Don as a 'weird little friend' before. He's going to fucking love you."

"Does it matter?" I searched his eyes. "It can be terrifying, I'm sure."

He leaned down and brushed his lips across mine. "Can I?"

I nodded, letting my eyes fall shut as he kissed me long and slow. His hands slid into my hair, massaging gently as I sighed. At some point, we ended up stretched out on top of his bed covers, making out like teens. I had no idea how long that lasted but my lips tingled when he removed my dress —again—and sank deep inside me, giving me time to get used to the feel of him, going slow for my aching, sore body.

And when I cried out his name he drove his hips harder, faster until the world blurred and only he remained.

The mafia prince I fell for one spring break.

Thank you for reading Falcon and Bella's spring break romance!

Read on for an excerpt of the next book in Rippton U Creatives- MAKE ME, BREAK ME

Make Me Break Me teaser

CHAPTER ONE

ZINZI

I woke out of my doze with a warm body behind me.

Fuck. I fell asleep. Again.

That was the problem with Dex Breaker—he was too damn cuddly. Who knew all that muscle was good for more than climbing him every time I got horny? I mean, he was damn good fun. He knew exactly where to find my orgasm button and just how many times to push it.

But he also knew my rules: get out before the sun

came up. Preferably midnight, too. No sleepovers, like ever.

Screw the Rippton U dormitory rulebook; we used my playbook, and mine alone.

I rolled into his warmth, pressed both hands to his hard pecs and gave a push. "Out. Get *out*, Dex. Of. My. Damn. Bed." I kept pushing until I rolled him to the edge of the mattress and tipped him off.

Thud.

"Fuck me, Zin. You play too rough." His gravelly voice did super fun things to my swollen pussy lips, the shape of him seared into my depths. Not to mention the cute-as-all-get-out sleepy eyes and mussed hair that still had my finger tracks in its curls.

All that gave me tugs in the heart strings department, which was why sleepovers were a great big, red flagged, no-fucking-*NO*.

"I have a rep for breaking my toys," I acknowledged, listening to the silence around us. The dorm was either empty—unlikely, midterm—or it was really damn late and I'd come too close to breaking my own rules. "Get out of my room. I need to sleep."

Dex crashed back to the floor with a groan at whatever he read on my face. "I'll sleep with you, babe."

I poked my head over the edge of the bed, my

dark hair tumbling haphazardly over my face in the dim reflected light from the union quadrangle outside my shitty little college room window. God alone knew what I looked like. Well, him and Dex.

"I'm not going to fall asleep with you or anyone else," I hissed.

"On the contrary, you just did. And your tiny snores are cute as hell. Half sn-rs. More like purrs, really." He winked at me, his come-hither, sexy ass smile curving sinful lips.

Sinful, because I knew just how much havoc that devious mouth could wreak on my body. Hell, I still bore evidence of his personal style, marks that I'd touch whenever the urge hit me midweek, reminding myself of the way he played us both into blissful oblivion.

"You're not leaving." I rolled on my back and covered my face with my hands, leaving my body naked and exposed. It wasn't like he hadn't seen everything before. "Why aren't you leaving?"

"Because I know what I can do with that stunning fucking body of yours if you let me stay." Dex got up on his knees and leaned over me to kiss me upside down.

His tongue invaded my mouth, tasting of him and me together because the slick bastard liked to lick me to one last orgasm once we were done for the night. He *always* had to have the last word.

Fine. If he wanted to play dirty, I'd play dirty. I kissed him back, lacing my fingers through his hair and scratching his scalp in the way I knew he loved. I knew everything about what Dex Breaker liked, but he forgot that in my hands, that knowledge was a weapon for me to abuse.

"Get going, or I'll cancel next Friday."

He broke the kiss and stared down at me in abject horror. "You wouldn't dare, you little hell cat. You know my Friday fuck sesh with you is the one highlight I can't go without. There's nothing like a boring week in the law department to make up new ways to torture that tight little body of yours."

"Oh, I will," I promised him, licking my lips. "Now get your sexy ass out my door before you break my rule."

Dex wrinkled his nose. "You and your fucking rules," he grumbled. "The fuck did my pants go?"

I rolled over to unhook his pants from one corner of my bed and tossed them at him. "Shirt's over the bathroom door," I said helpfully, not moving any further than I had to.

"We got raunchy huh, girl?" He pulled his shirt

over his head and yanked his jeans on from where they puddled near the door.

We never made it far before we got naked and filthy, in every sense. Dex made good work of my body. I'd be tender as hell tomorrow morning. Endorphins still coursed through me at high speed, leaving my legs liquid and my body floating.

I sighed as I ran my hands down my body. Yup, Dex knew how to show a girl a good time. I'd remember his fuck session right through to next weekend when we'd do it again and again. Every single Friday night, like clockwork. Or was that cockwork? The man fucked me into a brainless state. And now he needed to leave so I could function.

Despite my determination to be alone, my fingers traced through the mess on my stomach and thighs. How many times had he come on me? The sigh became a moan as I touched my swollen, over-sensitive clit. All movement at the door stopped as I played with myself.

"Fuck, that's hot," he rumbled in the sort of tone that indicated the randy law student was ready to go again.

Good feelings gone.

"Out, out, *out*." I threw both my pillows at him without looking at what I was aiming to hit.

Dex laughed as he opened the door. "Sweet dreams, Zin. Thanks for the night of debaucherous fucking sin." He laughed his ass off down the hall, apparently proud of his shitty little ditty—see, I could do it too—and likely woke the whole dorm.

Fuck them. I needed sleep and I needed it now. My head slapped the mattress before I remembered I'd thrown my pillows at Dex and the tall, muscular shit hadn't thrown them back.

Fuck my life.

Read Dex and Zinzi's enemies to lovers (when it's a Friday night and it's convenient) spicy dark MMA college romance story in

MAKE ME, BREAK ME

MERRY WITH A RANGER

A Texas Ranger Second Chance
Christmas Romance

CONTENT WARNING

For those who have been following TEXAN DEVILS for a while, Nash came to Rhys Archer as a troubled Texan boy reluctant to return to home soil. His story covers discussions on trauma, recounting of SA, family arguments, a little spanking kink and a few heavier subjects.

TEXAN DEVILS has often been a place where we don't shy away from tough subjects and in honor of Chuck who inspired this series with my nineties obsession of his show, Nash's story stays true to form. If you have triggers, we probably hit them here, but neither I as the author, nor any of my Rangers romanticize any form of trauma or hate speech or actions. Please read safely.

. . .

There's a Ranger out there for you.

Chapter One

NASH

This assignment was an utter waste of time.

I stared at the waves slapping the shore where the turquoise waves crested into golden sands with pale foam, and pretended I loved frolicking in the fucking sand like everyone else at Love Beach.

Then I cursed myself as a liar inside my own head before I shoved my toes deeper in the sand, praying for a thousand paper cuts to end the monotony of the first four days of my case here. The assignment I begged for with a different workplace and had it handed to me on a sandy platter in a new one.

But I didn't accrue the pain I needed as I linked my arms around my bent knees, letting my jacket hang around my body as I stared out the crashing waves. The cove would've been quieter than this overpopulated spot where tourists were desperate for a glimpse of heat in the midst of winter. A few days from Christmas, it seemed everyone in the destination hot spot tried to frolic in the waves while risking frostbite on occasion—okay, dramatics, but close enough.

But if I limited myself to a quiet area, my head would've been too loud.

Here, at least, I could hate on myself in the overbearing company of a hundred other cheery people who pretended to cover their own insecurities in brand names and out of season tan lines behind the shade of a giant, unlit Christmas tree that watched us from the boardwalk overlooking the ocean.

Love Beach was so far from Texas in every sense it wasn't funny. A state I never thought I'd return to, and the fact I did miss that patch of dirt imbued with so much sin and blood it wasn't funny that I almost laughed out loud. My heritage of that place disgusted me, but the job Rhys Archer offered me in return for a second chance at sanity on a place called home seemed like a good idea before a bomber blew himself back to hell with my grandfather's name on his lips.

The not so perfect welcome home present.

My teeth ground together as I fixed my gaze on some innocuous point beyond the horizon. The strange things that came to light when I wasn't looking. Or maybe it wasn't funny at all. Instead of seeing the details of what I should be picking out for this case, the only thing I spotted was the one person who could make this day better.

Or so much worse.

Depended on how fucked up my mind was when I reflected on it later.

Because the thing wasn't a thing at all, but a who.

Her. Bonnie Little.

I shouldn't have looked. Not even after ten long years, but I would know her anywhere. Still, I couldn't keep my eyes away from how her long, tanned legs peeked out from beneath the hem of her white sarong that flicked up every now and then to give me a tantalizing glimpse of her ankles.

No jewelry, because she never had been into that. It made buying her presents utter hell.

But I knew those legs. I knew those thighs, her waist, and hips, and everything else above her silky, filmy looking sarong that belonged to her. I didn't need to, but I dragged my eyes up her body anyway, torturing myself further with the girl who left me ten years ago without so much as a single word of goodbye.

The way body curved should've been illegal, enhanced from the last time I saw her. Pale blonde hair hung straight past her shoulders and curled at the ends just enough for man to wrap his finger around and tug before he drove himself slowly insane over that body hidden behind layers of gossamer wrapped around her. The rest of Bonnie Little was hidden beneath a white cardigan she hugged tight around her. But it didn't matter.

I remembered everything about the girl I fell for hard and fast and never recovered from.

What it felt like to kiss those soft, dusky lips that parted temptingly when she sighed. How she liked my thumb digging into her hip when I arched over her, and she submitted beneath me.

Everything.

Before she ran away and left me high and dry, wondering where the fuck she went at the end of our senior year.

The first girl I fell for. The only girl I ever loved.

I found her aqua gaze that matched the sea at the

same time as she flicked a wayward glance over her shoulder.

Those lips I could almost feel on mine, despite being dozens of feet away apart, hitched on a breath, stalling her easy gait. The chattering crowd that had disappeared for me rushed back as her lips silently framed my name before she picked up the material wrapped around legs and whirled away up the beach, away from me.

Nineteen year old Nash would've chased after her. Nineteen year old Nash would have demanded where she went the night she disappeared. The night when she blocked all my calls, and changed her number.

The night she ran.

He would have asked why she broke my heart, and never came back. He would have cared.

Today's Nash tipped his head back as I studied the way she darted away from me, already lost in a pensive memory of Bonnie Little I thought was long locked away behind wall with a plethora of cluster-fuck of one-night stands with all the other blonde women who never matched up to the shade of who she should have been in my life. I never could replace her, no matter how hard I tried.

Today's Nash let her go.

I dug my toes into the sand and finally achieved some of those tiny cuts I'd been trying for. Most of them were hardly scratches on the surface of my skin, but it was a start.

The corner of my mouth curled into a sadistic smile.

Bonnie Little could run, but in a town like Love Beach, she couldn't hide. Not for long. She had no chance. Not with me.

Not with an obsession that had been brewing since I last saw her ten years ago. No, this assignment just got a whole lot more interesting. Maybe Love Beach wouldn't be as boring as I expected.

I mentally flipped over the ring that had lived in my pocket since she ran away. Since I never got to give it to the girl who should have been my prom date, but when I went to get her, she wasn't there.

No, Texas could wait.

Sand etched its way along my ass crack despite the three showers I'd taken since I got back from the beach where I spotted my ghost girl who should never have been there in the first place.

The waste of water ingrained in my blood still got to me despite the years I spent outside of Texas. It didn't matter how much of the stuff floated around me or that I was back on the coast, for now. What had been bred into me couldn't be cancelled out on a whim, even for particles as annoying as the tiny grits that seemed determined to mine their way into every unavailable orifice.

But a few grits didn't change my focus as I sifted through files I knew by heart. Photos and names printed in blacks and whites, as well as color covered the resort bed. For the umpteenth time I worked back through the final night of a man's life laid out in front of me, but nothing could change the death of the bomber who knew information about my grandfather he took to the literal grave, albeit in several pieces.

When he blew himself back to hell in County, he left me with a message about the KKK grandmaster I hated who was still attached to my bloodline. I spent a decade away from Texas just to remove myself from the taint of my grandfather's actions, alienating myself from the family who still claimed me despite my pushing them away.

Even with the bomber dead and my grandfather whiling his final years away in respite care, I still scrubbed his sins from my skin daily even though they weren't mine.

Archer, my new boss at the Texas Ranger unit I'd become attached to when he offered me a position after the FBI failed to provide me with what I needed, had a penchant for manila folders and hard copy files. The resort coffee table and oversized, over-stuffed and unsupportive bed was covered with beige cardboard.

The man might be the cream of Texas Rangers down south, but right now I cursed him for his lack of ability to file a digital report like any other human in this century.

Not that Archer was old by any means; I was lucky if he had a decade on me. But from the moment I walked into his office, wary yet keen to accept a second chance and a reason to be back on Texas home soil, I could see the pain etched in his face that haunted the stocky Texas Ranger, his chestnut hair shot with occasional strand of silver.

His office was bare. Not in a rustic sense but stark enough to show he had no personal attachment to anything in it.

But I knew instinctively that it wasn't the things in his office, the tiny little space filled only with a scarred desk as old as the man seated behind it, and a row of equally marred filing cabinets that were the important things in the bigger picture to him. No, that would be the team that sat outside his office. Those were the critical factors in Rhys Archer's life, and that small fact instinctively told me this was a man I wanted to work for.

Especially when the first thing he did was hand me the one case we both knew I had chased for years, and would never refuse.

My grandfather's eyes stared up at me from the bed in a black-and-white photo. There were color ones of him that existed, sepia even, but I preferred this one. It showed a man in his prime, carrying that hideous white sheath in his unmarked hands. Glowing cheeks that, like so many psychos out there, didn't reflect the insanity festering within.

An insanity I feared might be contained inside me, too.

Not racism. I didn't give a fuck what my grandfather stood, or what sort of twisted moral PR agenda he pushed. That part disgusted me to the worst degree, and I wanted no part of it. No, the part of him that terrified me was that perhaps his darkness somehow passed down to me in some sick gene, and that no matter what I fought for, that part of him would always be a part of me.

That concept terrified me every damn day.

The rest of the local contingent of assholes pictured around him were either dead for the greater majority, or well into their eighties and nineties, living in nursing homes scattered about the state, unable to leave Texas if they wanted to. On the rarer occasion, the pictures weren't as pleasant, and some of my grandfather's cohort stared at the lens with accusing eyes like they expected the technology to steal their souls.

Okay, so for some of them their brand of insanity sat closer to the surface. I didn't glance at my own reflection in the small resort mirror, unwilling to see if my own insanity peeked through just yet.

My phone buzzed beside me. I tapped the screen without looking at it. A picture popped up in my periphery. Flicking the folder closed on my grandfather's face, I glanced across.

Archer: He left you a message.

The single line message accompanied the photograph. I stared at the collection of memorabilia spread across Archer's desk as bile rose into my throat.

Trophies were displayed in one image. My grandfather's personal collection. Proof of his life, his twisted *successes*, delivered courtesy of a dead man. Jewelry, a perfume bottle. Feather fans taken from someone's house he no doubt burned to the ground.

One of his favorite methods. I wanted to retch, but my eye caught on a picture of a pale hair comb just out of focus, similar to a gift I gave to a pretty girl once. But there were more. A diary, pens with men's names engraved on them.

Bowls of crosses, some with burn marks on them. A sickening orgy of evidence, more than I needed.

Everything I needed, beside the witness I'd come to Love Beach to find.

The case I'd tried to get myself assigned to for so many years and now I had it...the magnitude of the sins of my blood floored me. My skin wanted to walk off my bones as I stared at decades of destruction. No man, regardless of his age who had curated this much destruction in his lifetime, should be allowed to recline in a private nursing home with comforts denied by the lives of those he destroyed.

Swearing softly, I closed my phone, flipped all the manila folders over and tossed them into the box beside the bed away from the windows and threw a jacket over the top.

If this was what the assignment was going to be like, then I needed to find the bar. And maybe, my contact.

Two days later I was no closer in discovering the contact I'd been sent to Love Beach to find though I had created an intimate relationship with the bartender. It wasn't remotely close to dinner time, but there was a bottle of Mclellan on the back shelf I had a vested interest in, even if it bankrupted me by the end of the evening.

Throwing on a fresh shirt and grabbing my jacket, I ran my fingers through my hair and grabbed a piece of dragon fruit the housekeeper left in my bowl as an apparent imported Christmas treat. A weird pink and yellow thing with sweet, squishy innards, I'd become accustomed to them.

I headed for the exit, knife in hand ready to peel, when the heavy door shut behind me. I checked belatedly for my keycard—I hadn't locked myself out prematurely, bonus—and flicked the blade out, my mind already running back through the case that stagnated on me days in.

And breathed in a lungful of moonflower.

Bonnie.

That had been the scent she wore the last year we were together. My senses shut down, except maybe one. The single one attuned to her.

The same fingers searching for my key card in my pocket dug a little deeper, confirming the presence of something else there before I ripped my hand free and twisted around, but the hallway stood empty.

She's been here.

Fuck me, we were staying in the same place. The chances of that were... Well. In a place with a holiday floating population that swelled around this week and a limited number of resorts, the chances were high, to be honest. Somehow, I doubted my ex-Texas girl was a local. My heart kickstarted in my chest.

Discarding the desire to write myself off down at the bar for another unproductive evening, I leaned my back against the wall. Uncaring if I had to wait until she finished her dinner and drinks, I work on peeling my fruit no matter how long it took to find her again.

* * *

Fifteen minutes later she emerged on her own from a room across the hall from mine. A straw handbag hooked over her arm that looked like a basket decorated with seashells sewn on it. Bonnie wore a white dress that brushed the back of her calves and left a big scoop across her bare back. Risky with night falling, as the chill air picked up outside. Summer it might feel at Love beach year round, right up until the sun set.

The tiny edges of a tattoo peeked out beneath her white dress. I didn't need to see the full picture it represented to know the rest depicted half of a butterfly.

I knew, because the other half was tattooed on my hip. The two together matched to make the butterfly taking full flight. Individually, they perched on their branches, awaiting their other half, unable to fly alone. It was cliche, it was cheap. We were drunk, and teens when we had them done, and for the second time I emptied my bank account for this girl.

But of all the ink I later put on my body, that butterfly was my absolute favorite. No matter what happened between us, I'd never tattoo over it.

Rifling through her handbag and delving arm

deep as though she was Mary Poppins, Bonnie didn't see me until it was too late. I finished paring my fruit and put my knife up at the last minute as I stepped into her, my keycard in my hand as though I was heading for my room, not away from it. The deception should have eaten at me, but I was too desperate to have her body contact mine to care, already drunk on the idea of her.

"Heads up, okay, love?" I notched the flat of the blade under her chin, lifting her gaze to meet mine.

And stopped.

Azure eyes found mine and held for the second time in three days, and the floor might as well have dropped out from underneath me. The resort, too.

Christ. It's not meant to be like this.

Or maybe it is.

Somewhere in the crevices of my brain I recognized that I was supposed to be an adult, talk to her, etc., etc., But I was too far gone in her already to care. Her cheeks flushed the prettiest pink, her recognition instant as though my touch and voice was enough to set her off.

She didn't twist away, and I couldn't break my hand from her face, either.

That single point of contact, despite our proximity, stole my breath. Hers too, from the look of it. The sweet scent of moonflower drifted around us with her hair, a golden halo that brushed my shoulders with her momentum. One of her spaghetti straps fell down while she stared up at me.

All I wanted to do was lean and taste her, but that right disappeared the night she ran away from me. From everyone.

Where did you go? Why did you run?

Every question I once screamed at the night sky that never answered back sprinted to the forefront of my mind. But more than that, a flicker of something else darted about in those beautiful turquoise eyes a second before she shut down again, but I saw it.

I knew what to look for with her, because I knew this girl soul deep who was still etched into my bones as well as I knew Texas soil.

Fear.

Bonnie Little was afraid.

Of me.

"The fuck did I do you?"

Ten years apart, and that was the first thing I could think to say to her?

I expected her to run. I expected her to slap me.

Shove me aside, and run away screaming.

But Bonnie Little did none of those things. She shook her chin free of my blade, and stared up at me with those glossy pink lips still parted. Whatever she painted them with had a flicker of glitter in it I wanted to swipe away, get that shit off her. Underneath I could see the dusky color of her mouth underneath, the color I always loved.

But yeah, I lost that right a while back.

We were strangers to each other now.

And all I could think about was that she wasn't afraid of me in this moment.

"What on earth are you eating?"

I huffed at her. "I swear at you, and that's the first thing you say?"

She raised one shoulder, and dropped it. "I mean, it's been a weird day."

"Damn right."

A sweet smile creased her lips, but the expression was gone as fast as it came on with a practiced blankness I hated on her.

"It's dragon fruit." I sliced into the bright flesh to expose its monochromatic insides. "I shouldn't have asked what I did. I had no right. Not anymore." A tightness lodged in my throat I couldn't get past.

Bonnie nibbled on her bottom lip, took half a step back and fixed her dress strap, her fingers playing across her skin in a way that mesmerized me. "I was heading down to the bar before dinner."

"Drowning yourself when the ocean gets too much?" I didn't know where that came from. It was a stupid line.

"Something like that. Join me?"

I sliced off a piece of the fruit and passed it to her on the flat of the blade. She considered me for a moment before her lips parted. The dragon fruit disappeared as she licked my fingers when I pressed the offering between them, though I knew she wouldn't bite me.

Or maybe she would.

Strangers, remember?

A sharp breath sucked into my lungs. "Little Bonnie. Look at you, all grown up."

Her tongue flicked out to catch a drop of moisture that beaded across the lip gloss, missing my fingertips, though I wish she hadn't.

"Sweet," she acknowledged, stepping away from me and walking away down the hall. She didn't look over her shoulder to check that I followed her, nor did she need to.

She knows I'm all in.

I always was with her.

Chapter Two

B ONNIE

Nash Mercer hadn't changed at all. I mean, he'd grown a bit bulkier, added on about three tons of muscle, and there were more tattoos peeking out from his rolled up shirt sleeves and from his collar than when I left him more unmarked back in high school in our senior year. But other than that? He was still the same Texas boy with the sharp eyes who missed nothing and saw enough to land me in a whole lot of trouble.

Which was probably why it was a really good

idea to turn tail and run as far away from him as I could right now.

I wasn't sure why I wasn't running, like I did back on the beach. But right now, I didn't want to run. The last time I left Nash Mercer, I regretted it for the next few years until that, like all my other memories, numbed with time.

Or maybe I lied to myself, and nothing really numbed at all.

Not missing prom with the boy I hoped I might marry one day, have the whole picket fence, and all. Except in our world it was more likely a mansion than a picket fence. Or it was supposed to be. Two rich kids, neither of us from the wrong side of the track, who fell in love one summer and never got our happily ever after.

Maybe that's why it didn't work. Back then we had everything going for us. Before the world knew who his family was, and before my life...disintegrated.

One night, and everything changed. A simple dream of attending college together, getting married and living a stress-free life. What a joke. Nothing was stress free, but then kids think that way. At least, some do, for a short time. My over-entitled childhood was stripped away alongside my happy dreams that left me as cold and lifeless as the dim, ground floor resort corridor I traversed before Nash caught me up.

He walked along behind me for two floors, neither of us speaking. Ten years of non-history stood between us. I didn't know who he'd become in that time, and I couldn't tell him anything about myself. Whatever I said tonight would be a lie on top of more lies.

My eyes closed briefly as his fingers grazed my elbow, the flat of his blade still slightly sticky with the dragon fruit's pale pips from the sweet slice he offered me before.

And I took it straight from the knife that he slid between my lips, eating it with my eyes locked on him. *This boy makes me as mad for him as I was back then.* Before everything shattered. Our dreams, my sanity. My...everything.

But Nash Mercer wasn't a boy anymore. Hadn't been one for a long time, by the looks of him.

He flashed me a sideways glance without a smile, eyes dark, his face cast in sharp relief beneath the resort's bright overhead lighting that left him half brightly lit, the other half of him lost in shadows of his own making.

I was wrong. He had changed. I didn't know him anymore than I knew myself.

"What's Little Bonnie drinking tonight?"

He held the door to the bar for me, taking us from the bright white and blue downstairs halls to the darker lit, wooden based interior of the dining and bar area. I studied the giant Christmas tree—a real one, not plastic—trimmed within an inch of its life with crystalline snowflakes, hand painted, glittery baubles and perfectly tied burgundy velvet bows, lit from within with tiny, muted lights.

They glow on a strange frequency, not quite on and off, more a three on, one off, two on...it was an odd pattern. I stood beside him in the doorway, transfixed as I try to figure it out.

"I can see your brain working, love," Nash's low voice brushed my ear as he tucked my hair back. Rough knuckles grazed my skin, eliciting a shiver I wanted to hide from him. *Dangerous*. My mind screamed at me, but it was too late. I tried to twist away, but my feet rooted to the spot as his heat enveloped me, the door closing gently at our backs. "It's always been one of my favorite parts of you."

I forgot what he was talking about, and took a moment too long to catch up as he folded his body around mine like he was always supposed to be there. "Not that I ever got to use it." I clamped my mouth shut. "Sorry, that was stupid."

"Nothing about you is stupid." The hand that touched me glided lower to settle at the small of my back. "Drink?" That he ignored my faux pas and didn't ask questions was a relief. Like we'd fallen back into old patterns.

I closed my eyes and let him propel me gently to the bar. *This is Nash. I can trust him.* But also, this was *Nash*. I couldn't trust him because of who he was. Where he comes from.

Home.

I never got over leaving Texas. I'd also never been back. My last request that night was to push the driver to go back past the school, past the kids all gathered out the front for prom. My first mistake. My last, there. Because Nash stood apart from everyone, his brow furrowed, phone in his hand. Mine would have been pinging, back at home, but I wasn't that girl anymore, and she couldn't answer him.

His face raised, worry written all over the youth in him that died that day.

And some other part of me that I managed to salvage, that I held on to tight...that part died that night with him, too.

"What are you having, ma'am?" the bartender asked politely in that sort of tone that said it wasn't the first time he'd asked.

Nash's fingers flexed my back, and his sharp, indrawn breath said he was about to rescue me with an order he pulled out of his ass, as always. But I had my big girl panties on tonight, and I could save myself.

"Um, that one. Please." I poked blindly at a drink name I didn't recognize, and pasted a fake smile on my face.

My big girl panties were a silky white thong that matched the dress, and they were slipping.

"Doing good," Nash muttered under his breath, rubbing my lower back in a way that drew shocks along my spine. Literally no one had touched me that way, not since...

Well, him.

I swallowed hard, certain the bartender heard, but Nash's voice stayed low enough for only me to hear, apparently. I flashed him a grateful, if strained smile, and said the first thing that tumbled from my lips. "What have you been doing with yourself?"

"Professional surfer." His mouth tightened a fraction, enough for me to read the lie in him without checking him for tan lines...and I already did that back on the beach in a half second glance.

The only tan line Nash Mercer sported was one involving a shirt and tie outlined over his lying heart.

Don't know him anymore, my butt.

At least our deceptions matched.

"Surfer. Right." My words had a flatness I couldn't erase.

"Yeah." He swallowed, taking the whiskey the bartender poured for him, a double shot, and downed it in one. We had the same goal tonight, apparently. "You?"

"Elementary school teacher."

I took perverse pleasure in watching him choke on the overpriced alcohol and smiled innocuously as my own blue drink arrived, topped with an excess of cream, cherries, something that looked like sand from the beach, and a lackluster umbrella that refused to stay up.

From the look on his face, Nash knew just how that felt.

"Yeah?" He thumped his chest in an effort to breathe, his touch at my back wavering for just a second before he was back. His eyes zeroed in on me. "Happy with that career choice, Bonnie?"

The bartender made an excellent decision in heading up the other end of the bar to clean sparkling glasses.

I nodded and sipped my drink, failing in my attempt not to screw up my face with the excess of sugar. "Holy fuck," I whispered, loud enough for the bartender to snort up the other end of the bar, polishing away with an ardency I was sure the hotel manager would have adored.

Nash leaned in. "Bullshit tastes fine in that filthy mouth, huh, Teach?" His fingers trailed along my side as he sighed. "You know, I promised myself I was gonna try to take it slow with you, not get involved, all the right things, but..." He swiveled me around to face him in full, and there was no disguising the unslaked need in his eyes that reflected Christmas lights in all the wrong ways I suddenly craved. "You're making that damn hard."

I licked the obscenely sweet liquor off my lips. "My tongue is numb," I muttered.

He huffed, wrapping an arm around my waist and pulling me in close. "Got dinner plans, love?"

"My f– folks." My tongue played hardball, but I got the F word out, eventually.

Nash's face closed. "Your daddy's here? I wouldn't mind having a word with him."

My hair whipped my face, horror settling as I realized what he meant, but his attention already shifted. "No, that's a really bad idea–" Suddenly I was a seventeen year old girl with her life back in tatters, her arms around her legs trapped in a tatty t-shirt and a pair of ripped jeans that felt too tight and too big all at once while the rest of her class was dressed to the nines and her date grew angrier, like he did right now. "Nash, no–"

He turned on the spot, right as the door to the dining room opened, and my mother walked in, dressed in the same pants suit she'd worn to dinner every night this week. Her hair was done in the same way it had been when I was a girl. Nothing changed about her but for the vague expression on her face when she looked past me like I wasn't even there.

By now I was used to it. Nash, on the other hand, hadn't experienced my mother's mood swings where I spent the past decade growing used to them, *after*. They were my fault, after all.

My father, however—his sharp gaze lit on Nash and locked there.

"Good to see you again, son." His tone implied anything but as he glanced at me for confirmation that he hadn't started his own bout of hallucinations.

I nodded, detaching myself gently but there was no need. Nash's hand lay limp at his side.

"Daddy. You remember Nash?"

The two men stared at each other, both as stiff as dead men reawakening after an eternity beneath unturned Texas soil.

"Of course." My mother, so used to springing into action when needed though the brain cells long ceased to actually function, did so on demand as an automaton.

The shock of her Stepford wife-ish Mom-bot on his arm, her cheek upturned for her kiss, her blank expression, jolted Nash out of his stupor. A glance at me, and he leaned down to kiss her, murmuring soft, kind words to her ear though his flapping hand behind him gave away his freaked out reaction to the surreality of the situation.

I was the girl he should have taken to prom.

The girl who disappeared.

I had no idea what they all said afterward, but I read the hurt, the panic, the anger in his face that night. The abandonment.

I should never have asked the driver to take me past the school.

Daddy still didn't know about that. The detective took one look at my tear-stained face afterward, cursed enough to provide me with an extended vocabulary, and took me straight to the station like we should have agreed to much earlier.

That was the last time I saw Nash Mercer until that afternoon at Love Beach a few days ago.

I didn't know if fate brought us back together. I

didn't know if he could accept the person I'd become, but I did know one thing.

Tonight's dinner would be an utter shitfight—*if* he survived the questioning my father put him through afterwards.

I managed a faint smile, less than reassuring and all the things he needed as my broken mother retracted and headed toward the table in the corner we occupied all week because it appeared to be the only one in the room she could find.

My father continued to stare at Nash. After a while he held out a hand for the boy who never got a chance to say goodbye to follow the woman he refused to abandon when another might have.

Nash looked down at me, his eyes fathomless. Unchecked fury swirled in their depths. Tonight, I'd have questions to answer about our shared past, even though he didn't know that last part yet.

I didn't glance at Daddy, but I did keep my hand laced through Nash's as I followed him to our table.

Shitfight was absolutely the right term.

One of those words I learned from the detective that night.

Chapter Three

N ASH

Dinner was torture. Silent, pure death.

Thankfully, Bonnie chose the seat next to me, though her shell of a mother perched on my other side so I got the full blast of her father's interrogative stare across the table. That was okay. I understood him. Bonnie's mom, on the other hand...

Well, I understood her, too.

All too well.

I spent years in the FBI talking to traumatized women in various stages of recovery, trying to help them grasp details they barely remembered, or readying them for the stand in the hope that on the day they would be the performing monkey we all needed in order to put the sons of bitches who created the trauma away for a long, long time.

Occasionally, it worked.

Often, our processes created more damage than was there when we started. I hated it. Pinned between the two women, Bonnie with her innocent doe eyes staring beseechingly at me, and Mrs Little with her blank face that recognized no one, made the first steps to purgatory I earned myself dozens of times over for all the above reasons. Not that her mom seemed to know her husband or her child when Bonnie spoke to her across me, but somewhere in there Sarah Little recognized one thing: this conversation had to go on, and she was expected to be a part of it.

She played her role, just like everyone else at the table. Hers just came out a little more obvious, and stilted.

My heart ached for all of them, including the angry, protective father and husband seated across from me who seemed intent on ashing me with a single glare.

Unfortunately for him, that hadn't happened for me yet.

The moment my knife sat next to my fork across my plate he slapped the table decisively, jerking Bonnie out of her stupor where she shredded her paper napkin systematically into her lap beside me.

"Right. Nash and I need a chat on the balcony with a nice glass of that whiskey you were killing before we came in. Or three." His eyes warned me I wasn't taking Bonnie back to my room tonight, or any other night.

A twenty-seven year old woman who was fast on her way to becoming a mirror of her empty shell of a mother, in all respects. My spine stiffened, but I knew this conversation was coming the moment I saw him. To be honest, as much as I knew it would sting, my curiosity won out fair and square. Bonnie and I spent ten minutes at the bar earlier, lying our asses off to each other.

This man would slap me in the face with the truth for my own good and tell me to thank him for it.

I would, with a few hand selections of my own right back.

"Yes, sir." I rose, dragging my fingertips along

Bonnie's upper arm in full sight—nothing hidden here—anticipating her reaction.

She didn't disappoint.

Her shiver was a full body effort that left the scant remains of her napkin in confetti. A large part of me needed her beneath my weight the next time she did that, but first I had to deal with a different sort of threat who seemed to have no idea of the damage he did to his daughter.

"Two, please." My knuckles rapped the bar top lightly at the back of the room. The bartender didn't have a big job tonight; either everyone ate out, or the resort wasn't doing its job well over Christmas. "Event in town tonight?"

"Yacht party at the marina. You know rich kids. Plus the night markets on the boardwalk." His knowing gaze told me he recognized my ilk.

I nodded back and didn't ask him to throw his wisdom my way. Something told me I'd regret it. Hands filled with two generous fingers each to match the tip from earlier, I winked at Bonnie as she escorted her mother back toward the rooms.

Her lips sliding between whitened teeth, her gaze darted to the balcony and back. Hesitating for a second, she parked her mother in stasis near the door and the barman, and dashed back to me.

"I won't be that long." I searched her eyes, frowning.

"I never got to tell you anything." Her eyes glazed with more salt than the ocean beyond the closed doors, though a rushing far louder than the sea filled my ears the moment she started to speak. "I– there isn't enough time. Please find me afterward. I need to apologize."

"Bonnie, there's nothing—"

She shook her head, vehement. "You can't say that, Nash." One tear jeweled her lashes like a glistening Christmas bauble. "You don't *know*."

I swallowed hard. "You should have stayed." I backed up a step, and another as she mouthed two words that ripped me apart inside. The kid I'd been looking for her that night, and the man I'd been five minutes ago, still clinging to a futile specter of hope, died a little.

I couldn't.

Nothing else.

Turning my back to Bonnie, I paraded across the dining room floor to find her father outside and prayed I'd go numb in the night's ocean freezing air before he said anything else that stung.

Maybe I wasn't half as prepared as I thought.

Kicking the sliding door gently shut behind me, I

walked along the balcony where the wind picked up around the side of the building in a veritable gale. Naturally, that's where her father stood, his hands latched around the railing as though it would keep his bulk that was in no way threatened in blowing away on solid ground.

I coughed discreetly and passed over the glass. "Sir."

He took the glass without looking. There was a measure of trust I didn't expect.

"I know who you are, Mercer." He stared across the sand, up the long beach where white caps flickered further out to sea while the waves themselves were eaten by the darkness.

"I missed her that night." My voice stayed quiet, almost lost in the wind.

Almost.

He sighed. "We both did. She ever tell you?"

I shook my head, though he couldn't see the motion, and joined him at the railing, both our drinks untouched. "I spoke to her this afternoon for the first time in ten years, sir. Real gut punch. Thought...thought I was over her, you know. The disappearance. Don't know if you understood what happened after. The town was in an uproar. You all ran off. No one knew what happened. Speculation.

Lies, rumors...the works. Her name..." I shook my head and dipped my neck between my shoulders, stretching muscles that were never right after that night, but they weren't ready to give, yet. "I tried to quell them but I gotta admit even I struggled with that. After a while I got silent, too. Wondered where she'd gone. What happened to make you all run."

The words fell out and I cursed myself internally for being so verbose. The silent dinner hit me in all the right/wrong places. But as I glanced sideways at the father staring into the darkness, I knew I wasn't the only one affected that way. He just showed his fears, his stress differently.

Grant Little didn't move. Not a word or a breath escaped him, though he didn't hold back on purpose, turn purple or swell like an over puffed bullfrog. Nothing. That was a skill under duress. A learned trait. Or maybe this man endured so much that he'd mastered the art of stillness. An acquired skill.

"We were...required to leave." He spoke to the night, the wind whipping his words away the moment he spoke, but my trained ear picked up each one, already knowing the bullshit story he was about to spin for me. "Headed north, got out of town after my wife's first turn. Couldn't stay around after that.

303

Too much for her," he said gruffly, as though emotion caught up with him.

Or the lies of ten years eating away a conscience never meant for it.

I turned my glass in my hands and took a deep drink. Letting the pain then the smoothness roll through me, and found the best words I could, planted them on target.

"I used to respect you, sir." I stood side on so I looked him straight in the eyes, if only he'd face me but of course after that, he couldn't. "That was more bullshit than a rodeo clown deals with on a Saturday night."

Grant huffed at the air. What might have been a laugh died in his chest cavity. "Quick wit," he muttered. "She'll like that."

My throat tightened. *This is why investigations and personal life should never clash.* "I wasn't here for her," I murmured.

"No. You're FBI now, aren't you? S'pose you can't tell me the case you're working."

My eyebrows shot up, a response I couldn't curb if I wanted to. "Someone kept up with the local news," I observed, finishing my glass in one.

He eyed me, finally. "They teach you to drink like that, too, son?"

I snorted. "I started drinking the day I went to your house, found the door unlocked, and your daughter's phone on the bed, my messages and calls unread and unanswered. I woulda called the cops, but they were swarming all over your front lawn. You're the reason I chose that career, Mister Little."

He winced. "Lawson. It's Lawson, now. We... changed it. To protect my wife."

"Lawson." I sucked in that extra piece of bullshit and filed it away for later. Archer's cynicism was rubbing off on me. "I tried to open a file on Bonnie, but that got closed on me, time and again." I met his gaze, refused to back down.

You wouldn't have anything to do with that, would you? With your money and friends and power?

I didn't believe a word about everything being to protect the mother who took a turn. Sure, she was damaged as hell from trauma. I got that, loud and clear, and it was horrible. Bonnie wasn't the same, either. Something happened to them, but no one talked to me, then or now.

"So you could look for her?" he challenged.

"So I could stop what the fuck ever happened to her from happening to any other girl," I fired back. Swiping a hand through my hair, I shook my head.

"It doesn't matter, honestly. What happened, happened. I can't stop that. Hell, my family is a clusterfuck of its own." He stiffened, but I barraged on. "I only just got back to Texas after walking away for years. Finally got the case I wanted after all this time. Because the FBI wouldn't give it to me."

He frowned. "You're not FBI anymore?"

I shake my head. "Texas Ranger, brand spanking new." There was no keeping the pride out of my voice. I mightn't have been sure when Archer first called me, but I damn well was by the time I walked out of his office, hat and badge in hand.

Grant stared at me. For the first time the edge of his mouth smoothed out of the permanent frown it had lived in since he entered the dining room. "Not a bad career choice after all. What's the case you've been chasing all this time, then?"

Night air and sea salt filled my lungs on an inhale that made me wish I was back inside with Bonnie in my arms.

If she'd let me touch her.

"Taking my grandfather and his cohort out of their comfortable retirement homes and putting them into solitary where they fucking well belong. Lot of lives they damaged in their reign of terror.

Apparently one of my key witnesses is a local for the season."

Turning away from the horror on his face, I let the obsession that burned within my chest for too long as an ember take full root. *Consume me.*

"Thanks for the chat, Mister Lawson."

I turned away from the man I could have called *dad* if all the stars aligned and headed back to find his daughter, if she'd see me. If not, I had work to do. Sleep was meaningless after all these years.

I'd learned to live on little of it.

Chapter Four

BONNIE

Snores emanated from the unit next door that we rented. I locked the door between us, keeping my father out as I knew he'd want to talk—or rant—after he and Nash parted ways. Whatever their beef, I wanted no part of it. Those years were so long ago and yet still yesterday but the dread of it all followed me like I couldn't step away from it. From them.

Him.

And yet Nash was here. I wanted him near me, holding my hand like he used to, and asking me to dance with hope in his eyes and a tremor in his fingers.

But the Nash I met again forged his own path

and didn't have time for hope or simple things like dancing. And I was simply the forgotten girl whose childhood fell away before she became an adult who didn't get to play with simple dreams and things like hope any more.

Swallowing back the way of blackness that threatened to push me to the carpet, weighing me down. I forced one foot in front of the other, glancing back at the interlocking doorway that connected mine and my parent's room, knowing they would be furious if I left, but I hadn't been a teenager for a long, long time.

Nor, in all those years, had I claimed any sense of freedom or self at all.

Regardless, I still slipped out the door of my room with my keycard clutched in hand like I was sixteen, checking the hallway in both directions and ignoring the camera at the end of the corridor that wasn't recording anyway.

It couldn't be, when I was around. They made sure of it.

A familiar pressure built in my throat as I closed the door gently to an empty hallway. I made it all the way to the end, so ready to taste outside air, and walked straight into a familiar checked shirt and an unforgiving chest that most definitely wasn't that hard last time I had intimate contact with it.

"Your father is right behind me." Nash's brusque voice sent a riot of sensation along my skin in every direction, sweeping away the pressure and replacing it with something different. A shot of adrenaline I hadn't felt in far too long. His hands directed my body to turn, and I did, back the way I came. "Move it, Bonnie, or we lose any chance we have."

I quick-stepped it halfway up the hall, unsure if he was directing me back to my room or his, when his arm braced the wall before me and suddenly I shifted sideways into a stairwell I previously ignored.

"Fire escape." His lips brushed my ear. "Keep moving. Next landing, then stop. Okay?'

I nodded, my lips as unable to move as they did on that truly hideous cocktail earlier, or over that stilted dinner that killed every fraction of freedom Nash and I displayed before with our lies.

But this felt nothing like either of those moments.

A breath later and the fire escape door shut gently behind him. Nash's feet moved soundlessly to where I stood on the next landing under the cement stairs below. His fingers flicked sideways and I started on the next flight downward, halting in the shadows when he held up a hand.

My feet stalled. I froze as he took the next stair, stopping just above me, waiting.

Nothing. The door didn't open, nor did my father seem to know where Nash disappeared to, or that I was with him.

I opened my mouth, but his hand pressed to my stomach in a light touch. Light, but a warning all the same. *Count*, he mouthed to me.

I bit my lip, watching him, and counted in my head.

One Mississippi, two Mississippi...

By the time I got to five, Nash's body heat met mine on the same step. He wasn't bulky by any means, but his sort of muscle was still the solid sort, the type of man who'd be impossible to outrun.

This was Nash Mercer. If ever there was someone in this world to be terrified of, it was him. Because he knew me, and I couldn't hide from him.

But I wasn't terrified. Much.

My fingers brushed his collar, reaching up to find a few days' growth on his chin. "I like you like this," I mumbled into the darkness, unable to see his full face.

His hands braced against the wall behind me

over my head. "I was gonna take you outside. Wanted to walk somewhere. But it's kinda freezing."

"I like freezing." My head tipped back as I searched for his eyes, twin pinpoints of onyx in the roiling shadows he wore like a cloak. "Nash, what did he tell you—"

"Nothing."

"Oh." I swallowed, both relieved and back to being a little terrified at once.

"It's your story to tell, Bonnie Lawson."

Shit. My language really was going to get me into trouble with this man as I mouthed the word. His fingertips followed, tracing the movement of my lips. "What if I don't want to tell you?" *What if I can't?*

He shrugged. "Then you don't tell me. It's been a long damn time, Bonnie. Trust is built. Earned."

I could see the pain it cost him to admit that, but this wasn't just his story. "I broke that trust when we left. When I left."

"You were seventeen. There wasn't exactly a lot of choice. You were at school, Bonnie. A kid. We all were."

"I had to grow up pretty fast." I played with his buttons on his shirt, accidentally popped the top one open.

"Yeah?" His breath came fast, a little less regular

against my cheek. "You sure as hell look grown up to me now, Bonnie."

"I don't know if I am," I whispered back. "It's been a long time living like this, place to place, never stopping or settling..." I squeezed my eyes shut, but hot tears escaped anyway.

"Christ." One hand dropped to skate along my back, forcing its way between me and the wall. "You've been stuck like this for all that time..." The penny drops hard and fast. I didn't need to look at him to see it. "Fuck me. You're my—" He coughed into my hair, and the hand on my back dug into my skin beneath my dress. "You're in WITSEC, aren't you? Witness protection. Did your father Marshal up or something?" His dry humor fell endlessly.

I didn't bother to respond. "They're always watching. Just not...like you think." I leaned my forehead on his shirt and breathed in. Salt, whiskey and caramel. My cheek rested against his chest unbidden, and he let me steal a moment's comfort, still braced over me while his heart raced. "You're not a surfer, are you?"

He laughed, a hollow sound that rang around us. "Before this all gets shot to shit and I can pretend for half a second that I'm gonna have that picket fence with the girl I dreamed about for the last ten years, you gonna let me kiss you, Bonnie Little?"

He said Little. Not Lawson.

A sob tried to break free from my lips, but it seemed like Nash was done asking permission. His mouth found mine, his kiss as smooth as that caramel I scented on him before. Deft fingers wound through my hair, tilting my head to the angle he needed. I managed a long inhale on instinct before an all-male noise rose in his throat and his kiss changed into something darker, harder.

Whatever sort of picket fence Nash Mercer wanted, I was here for it.

His other hand banded around my waist, pushing me back into the wall. One knee speared between my legs, then the other, pushing my legs open to the limits of my dress. He cursed, freeing my waist to grip the fabric and yank upward. One hand settled on my thigh in a possessive grip that left me arching into him and his mouth returned to mine in fervor.

Hips grinding roughly into me, his tongue delving deep, Nash engulfed me until I swore nothing remained of Bonnie Little except an echo of a girl who craved a man she couldn't have.

But he was here right now, and I wanted him like I'd never been allowed to have anyone.

Linking one thigh over his hip, I levered myself up, clawing his neck as I kissed him back, sloppy and frantic and with no idea what the hell I was supposed to be doing.

"Damn, girl. You taste just like you used to. Texas summers and stolen midnights together. You remember those? I used to come and get you, drive you to the lookout and–" He pressed his body to mine in a slow grind I felt to my bones.

"Fuck," we whispered together.

"Girl, that mouth." His curled up in a slow smile that echoed to the tips of my toes. "Gonna get you in so much trouble."

"I remember everything." I tried to ignore the way my body lit up the closer he pressed until every-thing important evacuated from my body. *Air, blood, thoughts.* "Nash, I'm– I don't know what I'm doing."

He froze at my confession, those strong hands releasing me to press back over my head as his body arced against mine. "Say that again, love," he demanded.

But neither the words nor my mouth would cooperate. I shook my head, sucking my bottom lip into my mouth.

His gaze zeroed in on the movement when it popped back out. "Are you telling me—"

We teased and played with each other back in the day, back in Texas, but we were young, and he never pushed me for anything he didn't think I was ready for. Ever the gentleman, Nash Mercer, so before him, I remained a virgin.

I'd always wished he hadn't been quite so gentlemanly after all.

I blinked as his whole body backed off, and it became abundantly clear what he thought. "Oh, no. I'm not...you know. Innocent, or anything." I looked down, but that just left me staring at the straining bulge in his jeans. *Fail.* So I studied his rumpled shirt instead. "No, I mean, I've done— I've— I just don't know anything. That's all," I finished awkwardly.

One moment I was studying his shirt, the next I found myself in freefall in his eyes.

"Are you telling me that after ten long damn years of wishing I'd been the one to be with you back then, there's a chance I can still give you some of your firsts?" His frown was offset by the way his eyes searched my face, seeking answers I didn't want to give but needed to answer all the same.

I nodded, worrying my lip until it ached. "Mhmm."

Nash settled his body against mine, pressing in the damning rhythm again. "Words, love," he murmured, his voice a seduction all on its own.

"Yes, Nash. Anything I've got left to give is yours."

His mouth crashed down on mine, and ten years dissipated in a breath. He kissed me until my head swam with the scent of him, the warmth of his arms folding me into his chest twisted into the fabric of me that no one had ever been able to change no matter how caged and limited my life had been, all these years.

Nash snapped those tethers in seconds. Sliding his hands over my hips, he pulled me hard up against him, his thick erection hitting all the right spots as his body pressed into me relentlessly. I arched back, learning what he liked, a strangled whimper sliding between my lips to seek his mouth—

He pulled back with a groan and drew me down the stairs.

"What's going on?" I shook my head, dizzy from the change in tempo, swaying where I stood.

Nash cursed softly and drew me back to his side, pressing a kiss to my hair. "If I get to have some of your firsts, Bonnie, then I want one I never did back then."

"What's that?"

Letting him tuck me unto his side, I clung to him as we traversed the final stairs to the ground floor. He pushed open the door to the outside without setting off alarms, though somehow with him, I wasn't surprised.

"I'm taking you to the Christmas markets. And after that abysmal damn dinner, I'm buying you ice cream." He yanked off his jacket and tucked it around me, covering me in the scent of him, and hauled me outside.

Chapter Five

NASH

I was buying her ice cream. I didn't care if it was penguin weather outside. The temperate air of Love Beach turned icy as the wind picked up off the ocean and swept in like Santa Claus decided to bring the ice caps along for the ride this silly season.

With a day left to go before Christmas Eve hit—damn, I lost track of days hauling my ass across the country, then finding Bonnie—the entire population of the small town was out at the beachside night markets. No wonder the resort emptied of its floating population for the evening.

Vendors sold everything from gingerbread spiced lattes that scented the salty, sticky air with cloves and ginger and cinnamon. Giant Yorkshire puddings were offered by another shop. Hand blown, glass ornaments swung gently from all angels of a wooden hut, despite the wind, their tinkle audible where they dangled on long ribbons. Glowing neon reindeer, waving Santas, and other assorted Christmas light paraphernalia covered every inch of sand and board-walk as far as I could see.

Bonnie walked beside me, her hand wrapped around mine as she licked a vanilla—of all things—ice cream like it was the best treat she'd ever had.

I eyed her, willing myself not to get hard or grow too envious of the attention she gave a melting cone that was my idea to get her in the first place, and finally put words into action. "When was the last time you ordered dessert?"

Her eyes slid sideways, and I knew the answer to that before she said a word. "Daddy doesn't really allow it. Not unless it's one of those little biscuits that comes with coffee."

"Mhmm." The sound I made in the back of my throat came out rude, but Grant Lawson wasn't the respectful man I remembered from my youth.

Back then, I'd been afraid of him. I needed his approval to date his daughter, and I wanted to be worthy of them both. Now, he seemed to be afraid of me. The tables had turned. For some stupid reason, I preferred the status quo the other way around.

"Don't be like that." She finished the damn ice cream and licked her fingers, subjecting me to a fresh form of torture. "He does the best he can."

"How's that?" I didn't look sideways at her, and managed to keep my hand loose around hers.

Bonnie halted for a second but when I didn't stop with her she hurried to catch up, her pinkie still getting a suction clean in her mouth. "He's trying. You know, with Mom—"

I growled, frightening several market goers who gave us a wide berth as I spun on my heel, yanked the fingers out of her mouth and drew her close. "You can stop the bullshit about your mother. Yes, I get she's traumatized. It's horrible, Bonnie. But I've seen it enough to know that doesn't 'just happen', okay? Stop lying to me, and tell me what happened to you. Or don't. But don't expect me to believe the bullshit you've been spinning to the rest of the world and getting by on for the last ten years." I didn't step back, and I didn't give her space, knowing I pushed her way too hard.

Bonnie nodded, holding my gaze. "Okay. That seems fair."

The fuck?

"It does?" I let out a measured breath. "Bonnie..."

She held up a hand. "You gave me a choice. I'm taking the latter, for now. Maybe later, when we aren't...here, alright?" Her voice dropped an octave, begging me not to push her in public.

"Am I that much of an asshole you think I'll do that to you?" My mouth softened, and all I wanted to do was kiss her until the sun rose on Christmas morning.

Not practical, but then, closet romantics like me rarely were.

"No, I don't think that. Come on. I want to see the tree." She pointed shyly along the boardwalk to where a large tree was surrounded by glowing sheep, angels and what looked like dangling stars that wobbled only a little precariously in the high winds.

"You haven't been out to look at any of this?" I squeezed her hand gently. "Not prying. I genuinely want to know what you've done and haven't." And I was prying. But in the sweetest, least assholic way I could think to do.

"Nope." That was all the answer she'd give me, towing me along behind her as she wove her way through the small crowd that seemed to grow with the late hour, rather than disperse.

"Alright." I shrugged, following her until she

burst out into a clear area beside the giant tree that seemed to go on forever, even to a guy my height. "Hey." I wound my arms around her from behind, nuzzling into her hair. "We need a signal for every time something happens to you that you like and that's a first, okay?"

She laughed softly, scratching her nails lightly over the back of my hands. "What if I don't like it?"

I bit back a groan as her nails dug in a little, and I imagined her doing that to my back. "Then you gotta tell me so I learn you, okay? That's what trust builds on."

"I think we already have a bit of that." She breathed in, and pressed her body back into mine. "This. Now."

"Now?" I nuzzled into her hair, kissing the side of her throat as she made muffled squeaking sounds that drowned out the rest of the crowd altogether for me.

"Yes," she breathed, digging her nails right into my hands.

I pressed mine to her stomach, pulling her back into me. "This too?" I licked the slope of her neck and swore she fucking melted into me.

"Yeah, that," she said faintly, tipping her head

back to stare up the tree and the stars waving above us. "I don't want to leave here."

It was a child's wish, and for a moment her simple prayer stalled me. That's how cloistered her life had been. While I'd been screwing around with the FBI, making a career I was proud of, progressing enough that Archer knew my name and called when he had a vacancy, giving me a job in his Texas Ranger unit, and not buying myself the dog and house I promised I always would, she'd been...

What, exactly?

Living week to week in apartments with her mother and father watching over her shoulder. Living off their money and not having a life of her own. *Elementary school teacher my ass.* The stupidest thing about it all was that the girl in my arms had—has—the brains to do anything she wanted. She should have been prom queen. Valedictorian.

The girl I should have proposed to, after prom.

Instead I lost her, and she lost herself along the way, it seemed.

"Come back with me." I pulled her around roughly to face me. Her lips opened in a frozen 'o' as though she couldn't make the sound, but her pretty mouth framed it anyway. "Come back to Texas with me. I've got a rental place, and a new job. Needed the change, and it was time. I promised myself I'd buy a house, and a dog, but those things haven't happened for me yet. It's like I was...waiting for something." I swallowed my own wish. "Someone."

She stared at me, those blonde curls moving side to side, a negative on her lips, right there. I didn't want to hear it, and kissed her just to keep the pretense up for another minute. Slim arms wound around my neck as she pressed her body to mine.

"So...lots of surfing in Texas, huh?" She looked up at me through her lashes, calling me out on my bullshit point blank for the second time, unafraid.

This woman.

I grinned against her mouth. "Bit of a new thing. Had some things to wrap up here. But you're a pretty distraction." A lie. She was so much more than a distraction. At least, I thought she was from the indications her father gave me. But that was tomorrow Nash's problem.

"I can't go home."

Four words that ruined a future for us both. Just as I thought I had this life thing all figured out, fate sent me a moonflower scented curveball like her.

"Yeah? Where would home be?" I tucked her hair behind her ear. "What would it look like?" I pleaded with her, begging to know what she wanted. *Desperate.*

She shrugged. "I don't know. It's not something I can ever have so I never thought about it."

"There has to be something you want," I persisted, knowing I pushed her for all the selfish reasons now. I had committed to Archer's unit. Walking away was career suicide. But she was worth more than any career. Always had been.

"What I want." Her brow dipped low as she turned the idea over like it was a novelty. Maybe to her, it was exactly that. "I think...that white picket fence would be pretty. I don't care where, as long as it's with you." She leaned down after dropping that bomb of a pronouncement, and snuggled into my chest. "Oh, aneeeog."

"Huh, love?" I tapped the back of her head, then wound my fingers through her hair because it was too damn soft to avoid touching. "Say that last bit again." I was surprised that words came out at all.

She left me damn on breathless being so damn so close, saying all the things I wanted to hear more than anything in the world.

"And the dog. It's a good idea." She beamed up at me, and I saw what she did reflected in her eyes— an untouchable dream. A fairytale that wasn't real.

She'd stay in this moment with me, say what she really wanted because no part of her ever believed that it would come true.

Because that had been her shitty world since I saw her last.

Caged. Bound.

I needed to burn something or ash someone.

Instead, I gathered her close before the giant Christmas tree, the one with all the fake lights, and dangling stars, and dared to make a wish of my own. "What sort of dog would we have?"

"I don't know. I've never been allowed to have one of those, either. But I like big ones. The sort you can cuddle, but that you know will eat anyone who comes in that isn't supposed to be there."

I stared hard at the top of her head. "Aren't you full of the best sort of surprises, Bonnie Little?"

"Shh." She peeked up from her cozy place against my chest. "I'm not supposed to use—"

"Yeah, I know. Lawson and all." I sigh. "Don't worry, love. I won't get you hurt, okay? I get how it works."

The fact no one had come to rip her off me yet surprised me, but then maybe Archer put in a call. The man seemed to have an invisible and unending stream of clout that far exceeded his geographical territory.

She shrugged. "No one ever comes to see me. I just know they're there. It's scary. I hate it." She shivered in my arms, and I wrapped her tighter.

"You want to head back?" Another answer I knew. Maybe she was right about the trust thing. About knowing each other.

"Not yet." Decisive. Saying, not asking. We'd definitely established a baseline of trust even if it was forged on a decade of fairytale worthy hopes and dreams.

"Okay. Whatever you need, love." I turned her back around to stare up the tree.

We didn't move for an age. Not when the small choir of school aged children came by to serenade us, or the herd of baby reindeer paraded by, though she made cooing sounds. Or when a string quartet played a few carols before moving along.

Only when everyone started to pack up and the wind turned icy did she finally look up at me, the night's stars—real ones, not the fake—reflected in her eyes as she nodded and said, "I'd like to go in now."

So I took her hand, leading her all the way back to my room, and made sure I locked the door behind us.

Chapter Six

BONNIE

Nash's room looked as utilitarian as mine, though he'd likely occupied it for a far shorter time. Both our rooms appeared the same way: like no one lived here beyond the outward shell of us. My fingers trailed the basic bench bolted to the side of the wall, the matching TV that sat in my room.

A mirror image in all things, except for the box he kicked back under his bed the moment he flicked on the lights.

"Your father isn't gonna come in here and bitch slap me for stealing you away?" Nash muttered.

His back turned to me as he tidied the few personal belongings scattered across one small coffee table, reshuffling a laptop, a spare belt, some chargers.

Nothing I could use to work out who he'd become other than what I'd seen of the man himself.

He turned back to me, his fingers working the next button on his shirt, though he stalled when his gaze coasted along my body to reach my face. "Bonnie?"

I didn't realize I'd started to retreat until my butt bumped the opposite wall of the suddenly cramped room. "I haven't—"

He was across the room, standing in front of me, his hands flexing on my waist before I managed to expel my next breath.

"We don't have to do anything," he promised me, his words at odds with the need that strained his voice, reflecting in the darkest corners of his eyes as he tried to shut the emotion away, and failed.

"I said I would," I started, but he cut me off a second time.

"No. No way am I pushing a girl who says she wants something and then changes her mind. No chance. Especially not you." Nash's touch softened as he pulled me a little closer, still caging me in with his body, though his hold became less threatening. "Nothing you don't wanna do, Bonnie. Everything is your choice." His voice roughened, but he held my gaze with that same formidable, inner strength he'd had even as a wayward teen.

Not that Nash Mercer ever had a rebellious streak, exactly, more the exact opposite. Nothing ever got past him, much as right now.

"I understand," I whispered.

He nodded and lowered his mouth to brush mine in the lightest of kisses, giving me plenty of time to back away. "You want me to take you back to your room now?" His gaze stayed fixed steady on mine.

Whatever he felt inside, he showed nothing on the outside. Maybe that was part of whatever job he took on. At least we'd stopped lying to each other, if only for now.

"Not yet." My fingers twitched at my sides. Before I could question my own motives I buried them in his shirt, digging my fingers into his stomach in a way I was certain couldn't be comfortable. "I just froze up."

"Freezing up is fine." His thumbs skated over my ribs, through the thin material of my dress, beneath my borrowed jacket that still smelled like him. Whiskey and sea salt and Texas sunshine all at once. A terrible and beautiful dichotomy of all the things I loved and hated that left me homesick for a place I could barely remember. "Wanna watch something old? I have no idea what the resort has on streaming services." He backed off a step, or tried to, but my hands tangled in his shirt, stopping him. The corners of his mouth hooked up when I said nothing, and I didn't move an inch. "Gotta let go, Bonnie, or I'm gonna get the wrong idea."

I tugged at his shirt that loosened from his jeans, and found skin beneath. "So get the wrong idea." I had no idea where the daring words came from, but with Nash, even with that layer of hardness beneath that hadn't ever been there before, he was *safe*.

Safe, in a dangerous kind of way. The sort of man my father kept me away from for all these years under the guise of protecting me when really he just made a cage for a girl who wasn't seventeen wearing ripped jeans and getting a cop to drive her past the prom she couldn't attend any more, but wishing she was still intact like everyone else there that night.

His hands rose along my ribs, traced my upper arms and cupped my jaw. "Be sure, Bonnie. I'll stop any time, but you gotta tell me, okay?" he checked, staring straight through me, into me.

I nodded, licking my lips. "Okay." He said nothing, waited. "Okay, I'll tell you if I need you to stop or I feel...anything."

That mouth I needed on mine moved again. "Good girl."

Then he finally kissed me, his lips crashing sweetly into mine, and no matter what I promised there was no chance I'd be able to tell him anything at all because I never wanted that kiss to end.

So maybe I was still that seventeen year old girl at heart after all, at least a fragment of her, but only in this room, tonight, and only with this man.

No one else, not ever.

Just tonight.

Nash groaned softly as his arms folded tight around me, tucking me into his body. He fit perfectly against me, *still*. Even as a gangly teen he'd been the right size. Never too big, never so overpowering or overprotective that I felt like I'd disappear and never be seen again, overwhelmed by the sheer mass of him.

Even when he kissed me on the beach and engulfed me before, I knew it was only temporary. Nash never stole my identity, took any part of me away from myself. That's what our trust was based on. That, and we *fit* together. Just enough that I knew he could wrap himself around me, hold me up if he wanted.

That sort of strength, along with every other part of him, was sexy as hell. His stomach contracted beneath my fingers as I rediscovered the flat planes of muscle there as well as some scars that hadn't been present before. The landscape of him might have changed over the years, but the way he kissed me, hesitant in hurting me or pushing too hard, too fast, but wanting to go that step further, both of us—that had always been the same.

The difference was that after all this time, I was ready. Truth be told, I'd been ready then. It just took a catastrophic life event for the child in me to be stripped away to recognize that.

But that same girl had a chance to reclaim something tonight.

Nash's kisses grew rougher as he pushed his tongue between my lips, searching for a deeper touch. I arched against him, desperate for the same intimacy, fumbling his buttons with an unsteady hand. My breath shattered against his lips as he laughed softly, a dangerous sound as he scooped me off my feet and lifted me over his bed, yanking back the covers with one arm.

The lights flicked off, leaving us half lit by the giant Christmas tree's ambient glow outside his window. It was plenty enough to see by, and the warm light left me able to hide, better than the bright down lights.

"Is this okay?" Nash slid his hands under my jacket, pushing both it and the straps of my dress off my shoulders.

My throat worked on nothing at all, and I managed a nod.

"Words, Bonnie." His voice whipped out at me like a slap. I recoiled on the bed, scooting back but he arced over me, boxing me in with his forearms planted beside my head, spreading my legs with his knees. Suddenly, the bed seemed like a threat of its own. "Give me those words you promised, Little Bonnie, or we're going to have a problem." His mouth dipped to trace a line along my collar bone, removing the possibility of speech.

I fell back to the pillows beneath my head, collapsing into a nest made of the scent of him and his scrunched jacket as his weight settled over me. His body pressed into all the right places as I hooked a heel behind his knee, kicking off my shoes.

"I like that," I whispered as he licked and kissed along the hollow of my throat that seemed intent on creating noses of its own.

"I remember." Nash ran a hand down my body to settle at my hip, tugging my dress to my waist. "You know the one fantasy I've had for years that we never played out? Taking you out to the bleachers at the sports field on a sunny afternoon when no one was there, laying you back all bare—" He brushed his palm beneath my dress to discover my silky thong and made a growling sound in his chest, "—take these off, and lick you until you creamed all over my tongue. Then fill you and love you in the sunlight with no one around. Just us. Find out what it felt like to sink into you while you moaned for me, all hot and wet and dirty." He stared down at me, his eyes black and fathomless.

My traitorous body throbbed and clenched on nothing as he cupped my pussy over my panties. "That's a good fantasy," I managed.

His fingertips pressed right over my entrance, no doubt feeling the heat emanating from me at his filthy words that were beyond a turn on because I could imagine him doing exactly what he described just fine. It was the place we shared our first kiss, and even that turned a little X-rated by accident. He'd been a gentleman then, but then heat in his eyes both scared me in all the right ways and turned me on then, too.

So long ago.

But not so long, after all.

"You like that, huh?" Nash pressed in, rubbing my satin panties over my wet pussy.

Swallowing hard, I met the challenge in his eyes. "Show me what you'd do if we were there now," I begged. "Please, Nash. Take me back there tonight."

"Fuck, I love that mouth on you." He bent down and kissed me hard until my lips throbbed, his tongue invading my mouth until I couldn't breathe for the scent of him overflowing my senses.

Even if this was a one night thing, he was imprinted into my brain, my body—and a whole lot deeper—forever.

Nash ran his fingers along my dress and paused. "I wanna rip this right off you, but getting you back to your room and explaining might be tough," he said in a low, strained voice. "If you want me to show you my party trick, I want you to strip for me, love."

I shivered under his lustful gaze. "I—what?"

His lips curled up sinfully. "Tell me you've never watched a dirty movie before, Bonnie."

My cheeks flamed. "Stop that."

"Right. So." He rolled to one side, rubbing his fingers along my stomach. "I want to see you," he whispered, grazing his mouth against my cheek. "You're so fucking beautiful. Show me every part of you."

This was so far outside my wheelhouse that we'd left the realm of amusing behind long, long ago. But if this was what he wanted, then the people pleaser in me needed to try. Hell, the Nash pleaser in me wanted to try, as well. But my cheeks still flamed as I pushed myself up into a pretzel, his jacket hanging off one shoulder, my legs tucked beneath me.

"I have no idea how to start," I admitted.

His gaze coasted over me as he hooked one finger into the back of my stolen jacket and tugged gently, forcing my shoulders to roll backward, pushing my breasts forward. My head tipped to one side as I watched him, and his mouth brushed over mine.

"That's a damn good start," he breathed.

I let him tug the jacket free, and raised my hands to the dress straps he started on before, slowly sliding them off my shoulders. His eyes tracked that movement too, hunger edging into them as I reached back and started to undo the back of my dress then stopped. I had no bra beneath, which meant I really had to stand up for this next part.

My mouth dried, but it was a now-or-never type decision. Sliding off the bed, I turned my back to him, barely daring to glance over my shoulder. Nash watched me with lazy but heated eyes, his hands resting on his thighs. I slowly lowered the zip in my dress and let it slide to the floor, leaving me in that white, silky thong.

His sharp inhale told me I didn't screw it up, and managed to hook my thumbs into the side straps, wiggling my feet hip width apart and bent forward at the waist, tugging the elastic down. I barely got the panties past my ass cheeks and didn't have to worry about the rest of the mechanics when his hand came down firmly on the small of my back.

"Don't move," Nash said softly, leaving his hand there, though his other traced the curve of my buttock, then a little lower, finding the first drips of dampness and spreading them around.

A whimper left my lips. He said *don't move*, not *don't make any sounds*. I couldn't help the noises that slipped from out as he played with my wet pussy, discovering the shape of my swollen, slick folds, how I shivered when he traced over them, pressed his long fingers into me.

The moment I cried out when he pushed two fingers deep into me and worked them fast he cursed, his hand on my hip gripped tight, before that touch disappeared. His hand closed lightly around my throat, levering my upward.

"Bonnie, you're gonna have to tell me if I can fuck you like this or you want to be back on the bed right now because damn, love, you are far too tempting like that."

He twisted my head back so I had to look at him. My body jostled sideways, and his hand between us rubbed his erection in long, slow strokes that matched his labored breathing.

A sense of power that I'd done this to him, after so long apart, slammed into me.

"However you want, Nash. Just—go slow for a little bit, okay?" Something in my face must have shown through as he cursed again.

A breath later I was on my back with him above me, my thong discarded with the rest of my clothes, alongside his.

"What–?" I swore I wasn't going to get a full sentence out tonight.

"Love, I promise I'll show you everything. But for your first time with me I want to stretch you gently, okay?" His hand found mine and closed my fingers around his—

Girth. Not length. He was worried about actually hurting me.

"Oh, shit." Not eloquent, but it was all I had right then. "I'm more breakable than I thought."

He laughed down at me gently. "Not the way we'll do this, if you're still okay with it. I promise you've gonna like it. But you held up your end. Now it's my turn to take care of you."

Nash pressed me back into the pillow again. Breath whooshed out of me as he slid down my body and between my legs. Then his mouth settled over my bare skin below where I waxed for the beach because I liked the idea of wearing white dresses and white bikinis, never thinking someone else might see me bare.

"Christ, love," he muttered reverently, licking and nibbling on tender flesh. I found his hair and tugged on the short ends, scraping my nails along his scalp as he groaned into my damp skin. "This night is gonna make my top two."

He latched onto my clit at the same time as his tongue dived into my core and I screamed into my fist.

"Oh, God. What was the first?" I panted.

He paused and looked up at me, his brow

furrowed. "You don't know?" I shook my head. "Naughty Bonnie," he reproved me in a low voice. "We can deal with that later. The top night is when you got drunk and told me you loved me over a text message back in the day. Best fucking night of my life."

My eyes filled with tears. I tried to answer him, but nothing at all came out. He didn't seem to mind, only went back to the task he set himself, licking and eating me until my legs shook, and he hooked my thighs over his shoulders.

I screamed a second time into my hands, clasping them over my mouth, my heels drumming into his back. Tears cascaded from the corners of my eyes as I came hard.

And the whole time, he never took his eyes off me.

His mouth full of the taste of me—I knew because he climbed up my body, kissing me long and sweet afterward as he rolled on a condom one handed—Nash pressed his thick length at my entrance and pushed in. My fear evaporated by then, and I wound myself around him, my body and heart welcoming the man who held me together over an entire decade, showing me pleasure and pain, adoration after emptiness.

He started slow, but Nash never did anything

sweet, not all the way. That edge of danger was always present, always there with him. Once he knew I was alright, his hips slammed into mine as he claimed me over and over. I kissed him back between the noises he bred from me, finding how our bodies and souls fit together after all that time.

This time when I screamed, it was his name into his chest as he cradled me tight to him. I licked the salt of him away as I came down, but he wasn't done. Determination lit his darkened eyes as he marked me inside and out as his. I clung to him and rode the overdose of pleasure out, my mind a splintered mess only holding on enough to hear what he whispered, his lips pressed to my sweat-slicked skin before he roared my name over me, his grip as possessive as his last kisses as the sun rose and the fairytale shattered.

Three words I would cling to no matter what came next for both of us.

"I love you."

Still.

Chapter Seven

N ASH

We both knew she couldn't stay. Bonnie dozed beside me, one eye on the cheap bedside clock that went off the first night I stayed in the resort at the wrong hour that someone who stayed in the room before me set for some ungodly time and forgot to change before they left.

I promptly reset the thing and forgot about it. Now, I hoped the damn thing failed and never went off ever again.

Bonnie shifted, rolling to face me. "I can feel you watching me," she murmured with her eyes closed.

I trailed my hand along her waist, over the curve of her hips, though she was so slight, there was barely anything of her. I swore I'd change that, at least a little. What her father did to her...he might try to protect the women in his life, but in his desperation he'd become selfish and cruel.

But that wasn't her worry right now.

"So beautiful." I leaned down and captured her mouth with mine, kissing her long and slow, savoring the sweet taste of her. All stunning and innocent, no matter what she seemed to think.

Years too late, I got the second chance with her I needed, always craved, and never expected to earn. Bonnie sighed beneath me as I pulled her in closer, discarding the notion of time or her father, or her watchdogs. Fuck them all. Right now she was mine, and I refused to give her up.

"Happy Christmas Eve," I murmured against her mouth.

"Is it?" She stared up at me, confusion creasing fine lines around her eyes.

Somehow that made her more beautiful. I wanted all the years with her we missed in between and swore to her and myself silently in my head I'd find a way to make it work for us. Now I had her in my arms again, there was no way I'd let her go. Bonnie Little was the best Christmas present I'd ever had. If I had my way, she'd be Bonnie Mercer come the new year.

If she let me. But by the way her lips twisted prettily as her mind caught up said she wouldn't push me away. At least, not right now. Neither of us put on clothes after I fucked her into the mattress earlier. What started slow blew out fairly fast, which meant I owed my girl an apology.

But when I pressed her onto her back, settling my weight over her, Bonnie's hands shoved lightly at my chest. I backed up in a hurry, and it was my turn to frown. "Did I hurt you? Scare you?" I checked in, cupping her face, pressing my thumb over her pulse point, but her rhythm remained steady, and slow.

"Nope." She popped the 'p' softly, shaking her head and pushed on my chest again. "Off." When I still didn't move, staring down at her intently, she clicked her tongue, the only sign of impatience she offered. "Nash? You got your fantasy time in. Now it's my turn."

Finally, a smile spread over my lips. "You got it."

I kissed her again as I peeled my body from hers, barely able to keep my mouth off her, sliding my tongue along hers.

She moaned as she let me roll us, settling her body over mine, her thighs spread to straddle either side of me. When I opened my eyes she sat over me, her dripping pussy rubbing gently over my cock that knew her heat like its own. I caught her hips, but she swatted my hands away, her eyes glowing.

"No, I want to do this myself."

Swallowing back my need to control each grind of her hips along my stiffening length, I tucked my hands behind my head, lacing my fingers together with a supreme effort of willpower. "I'm all yours, love. Anything you want to do."

"Anything, huh?" Bonnie rocked gently against me, slicking me with our mixed fluids, and earning herself a groan from my lips. I couldn't hold back if I wanted to, and there was nothing I wanted to hide from this girl.

The way she looked at me made me wonder if I hadn't just thrown myself in the deep end, but how much trouble could an almost-virginal, twenty-some-thing cloistered ex-girlfriend be?

The moment she slithered along my body,

gliding those kiss-bitten lips over my cock and licked my balls, I knew I was screwed. Or about to be.

I should have studied the ceiling. The light fixtures. An errant, missed cobweb.

Instead, I watched her lashes sweep over her blush-stained cheeks as she explored me like we never got to do back then. Before our worlds were thrown into a maelstrom of uncertainty and separate hells.

My breath shuddered from my lungs as I scratched vicious patterns into my scalp where she couldn't see, desperate to wrap my hands in her hair and fuck her pretty little mouth until she sobbed and choked for me. But I promised I'd let her have her way, and I was a man of my word.

For now.

Bonnie graduated from exploring my thighs and everything below my cock with her tongue and hit the main event, fitting as much of me in her mouth with one swallow as she could.

I swore I drew blood on the back of my neck. A long hiss burst from my lips as my legs stiffened.

She broke her concentration, looking up at me, her mouth stuffed full of cock, lashes obscuring her eyes as her tongue flicked over my cock head. My balls drew up painfully tight as I willed myself not to paint her tongue with my seed, desperate to feel her sink down on me once she finished torturing me.

Finally she released me, her lips pinched. "Am I doing it wrong?"

I released my hands from behind my head, relieved to see no blood caked beneath my nails, and crooked a finger. "Come here," I ordered softly.

She crawled up my body, hovering over me. Her hair draped across my shoulders, tight nipples grazing my pecs. "Tell me what I did?" she begged prettily.

I caught her chin in a firm grip. "What you did was nearly make me come in your mouth, love," I admitted, freeing up my other hand to swat her ass.

She squealed in a delayed reaction. "Nash," she gasped a breath later, clawing my shoulders.

I smirked. "What, daddy never smacked his princess?"

Her gaze lowered. "You know he didn't."

I found her glorious tits and toyed with them until she panted, twirling the nipples between forefinger and thumb and tugging her closer. "That's alright, Bonnie. I'll pick up what's been left out. Make sure you're looked after. You need another?"

I pinched her nipple slowly, not too hard, but hard enough. Letting her feel the pain develop, I kept a hold until a second after my name left her lips again.

Hesitant, she met my eyes again and nodded, just once.

I urged her closer and tucked her into my body, sweeping my hand over her ass where I spanked her before. When she breathed out, I planted my palm in the same spot, a little softer on her already warmed flesh. She didn't jolt as much this time, but her heat increased over my groin.

"Say thank you," I murmured against her cheek, tasting the dampness of her tears. "It's okay if you need to let it out. You've been living a fucked up little life, love. Anything you need, I promise I'll give it to you."

"Thank you, Nash. Maybe, just one more? The other side. Please," she added belatedly.

"My pleasure." I kissed her sweetly for begging so well, sliding my tongue along hers, then drew back to watch her face as I spanked her hard on the other side.

A single tear trickled down her cheek as she trembled for me and let out the most beautiful, relaxed sigh.

I swept the salty drop back with my thumb, pressing her tear to the corner of her lips. "Taste,

Bonnie. That's your freedom. What you take," I reminded her. "Every step you get is for yourself. Can you breathe?"

I held her close, wanting to roll us both and slide inside her, but I promised her, and dammit that oath was gonna kill me.

"Yes," she whispered. "It's not so impossible now."

"God, you're fucking beautiful." I kissed her again, arranging her how she was when she started. "You said you had a fantasy. I can take over if you need. Whatever you want, Bonnie."

Her hands played with my stomach, tracing over the scars there, some of the old knife and bullet wounds I earned in service. Some cops went years without drawing a weapon. I put myself in the line of fire the moment I earned my badge because I couldn't sleep at night if I drove a desk all damn day. Lost thinking about her, never allowed to investigate her case.

Until now.

And all I wanted to do was take her away from it all, throw my career away and run with her somewhere nothing else mattered but her freedom.

Fuck it, after Christmas I might do it anyway. The whole vengeance thing no longer mattered anywhere near as much as it did when I arrived at Love Beach. The box of files under my bed burned a hole in my back as she straddled me, some of her confidence regained with her glowing behind.

Bonnie let me grip her hips this time, helping guide her as she caught my cock in her hand and raised herself over me, then slid down my length, her heat enveloping me until we both moaned, entangled in each other's arms.

And I forgot everything except for the soft girl wrapped around me, her breasts pressed to my chest, her heart beating too fast with mine. Bonnie worked out how to ride me while I tried my damndest not to coat her walls with the pleasure of being bare inside her. Too late the thought ran through my head, but the moment I tried to shift, she shook her head, recognition crossing her face.

"Implant," she whispered.

I swallowed hard, finding her ass cheeks I spanked before and bottoming out in her in one go as I levered myself up to press my back to the bed's headboard. "I'm clean, love. Are you sure?" I searched her face. "I know I promised, but I'm not a god. And you feel so fucking good I just want to rail you into the bed until my name is the only thing on your lips."

Bonnie's lips parted a fraction, her breath kissing my cheeks. "Do it," she whispered.

We never go that far.

I slammed her down onto my cock, her ass a two-handed grip as I pounded into her swollen, needy pussy from below. Over and over, until she cried my name on repeat into my ear. The soundtrack I came to, my neck straining, still not letting her go as I fused our bodies together and filled her to the brim.

My orgasm hurt like a fucking truck smashing into me, ripping my insides out, the lines of pleasure and pain melding. The only thing I felt after was her heat wrapped around me, her body trembling after the way I railed her. And finally my senses came back to me.

"Christ, tell me I didn't actually hurt you," I muttered, pushing her hair aside until I found her face tucked into my shoulder in a pool of sweat and saliva. "Bonnie. Love?" I cupped her chin and tilted her head up to mine.

Her makeup smeared beneath her eyes, her cheeks stained a violent red as she panted gently.

"I'm good," she whispered. "Just...wow. Are you like that all the time?"

I laughed, resting back against the wall, half

expecting the bed to collapse beneath us both at any moment. "Just with you, love. Only you."

I stroked her hair, tucking her back where I excavated her from and managed a breath. The time, the clock, the world was all forgotten as we came down from the incredible high of falling into each other again and finding out we got it right the first time around.

Chapter Eight

N ASH

When the threat came, I had all the timings wrong. Bonnie and I managed to spend the morning in each other's arms without incident until the door to my room was kicked in without any prior announcement.

"That's just fucking rude," I muttered as I rubbed sleep from my eyes with one hand and tucked her beneath the blankets with the other, figuring her father would at least knock.

That was the part I got wrong. Not the knocking, her father.

Because I found myself looking down the wrong end of a gun no one ever wanted to be on, and I'd had enough of that particular end for a lifetime.

"Fuck me." I pushed Bonnie behind me as I stared at a man I didn't know who hadn't bothered to cover his face, and that fact alone boded really shit-tily for the start of Christmas Eve for both of us right when I found the first spark of happiness in a long damn time.

The second part of it was that while his gun was pointed at me, his attention was on *her*.

"Get out," he snapped, as though he expected her to know him. "I'll deal with you shortly."

I couldn't risk taking my eyes off him, but the way Bonnie stiffened behind me, then shifted away, told me I miscalculated really fucking badly.

"Love, I need you to use those words you promised me before," I murmured, gliding my hand under my pillow for the gun that should have been there, but wasn't.

Where the fuck is it?

"I'm sorry, Nash," she replied, her voice way too steady for my liking. A metaphorical sucker punch hit me in the back, right in the damn kidneys, and stole all my air.

"Sorry for...? Give me something more," I muttered, more than a little desperate.

"Sorry for this." Sadness filled her voice, enough that I risked turning to look at her.

In time to see her raise the handgun I was missing, flick the safety expertly off and double tap the asshole holding the gun on us.

The fact he never fired before he fell, never made a single sound, told me he expected the move less than I did.

I didn't turn around to check. She hadn't missed, not at that range, not with that confidence or skill level. My cock stirred at the image of her burned forever into my mind holding that gun, naked, her legs spread apart, fierce determination written across her stunning face even as my eardrums protested at the noise abuse.

"Damn, girl. If this is how I die, I'm good with it," I breathed when my head stopped ringing.

She managed a hiccup as she lowered my gun. I caught her as her knees bent, collapsing beneath her. The gun tumbled from her hand. I caught that too, flicking the safety back on, and sliding it beside the box under the bed. Then I tucked her into my side and wrapped the blankets around her as she began to shake, her brief spurt of adrenaline leaving her as fast as it came on.

"Never actually taken out a live target before, huh?" I kissed the top of her head. "Proud of you, love."

She hiccupped amongst the sobs. "You have?"

"Yeah." I huffed out a laugh. "Couple of times now. Still feel shit on the inside no matter what I pretend. Wanna tell me who taught you to shoot like that?"

"I did."

The knock I expected still didn't come, but with the door kicked in like that, who needed to knock?

Grant Little-Lawson stared back at me when I turned my head, then his attention dropped to the body on the floor. "I'm sorry it had to be you."

I figured he wasn't talking to me, or the dead man staining the carpet. "Someone gonna tell me why I got a dead body on the floor and why I have to explain to my boss why my gun was fired by someone who isn't me?" I didn't let go of Bonnie, and she still shook in my arms beneath the sheets.

Grant made the wise choice not to comment on the fact that we shared a bed, nor our state of undress. He did, however, need to start talking, or she did, because resort management and the local cops were going to be up our combined asses in a matter of minutes.

As much as I enjoyed being a Texas Ranger, that shiny little star didn't mean shit halfway across the country. For the first time since I resigned, I missed my FBI badge with a vengeance.

"I want to tell him."

Bonnie's voice came from the region of my armpit. I tugged gently on her hair and ignored her father who didn't scare me half as much as he had when I was a kid.

"Love, if you want to tell me your story then you'd better hurry up. We have a very limited time before I'm going to need to explain myself and put pants on." I paused. "And we should probably move to a different room." The small living area off my bedroom would do. While I was used to the aroma of death, I doubted Bonnie had that life experience.

Grant sighed. "I'll run interference. Buy you a few minutes. Best talk fast, Bon-Bon."

I carried Bonnie to the two-seater sofa, still wrapped in the sheet, collecting our clothes as we went.

Her fingers flicked at my side, nails scratching my ribs lightly at the nickname she never told him she hated. "I'll be quick," she muttered, tickling me with her breath.

I waited until Grant left the apartment, positioning his bulk with his back to the doorway so no one could see in, and hauled her out of my tickle zone to slam my mouth down on hers. "That was the sexiest fucking thing I've ever seen, love," I murmured into her mouth.

Grant coughed not so discreetly from the resort room doorway.

Bonnie grimaced, ignoring both him and the dead man congealing on the floor behind us, but at least we didn't have to breathe him in now.

"I need clothes," she whispered.

My arms wrapped around her middle as I hauled her against me. "Right now you need to tell me what the fuck happened." I captured her jaw between my fingers and fixed her with a hard stare. "I'm not gonna leave you to face any of this alone. I'm not leaving *you*, love. But I need information, because I can't protect you without that."

Her mouth made the sweetest little moue without her knowing it, I thought, and I kissed her before she could say anything. Hands swatted at my shoulders until I gave her air.

"I can't talk if you do that," she hissed. "I–"

Her gaze darted to the door, and my arms tightened. Breath left her, and it was like her entire body deflated. I knew she wasn't ready to talk but we'd run out of the luxury of time. Her heart rate picked up against my arms as I pressed my lips to her temple and promised I'd make love to her at some future point.

Sometime. When I could contain myself from needing to screw us both into next week. Month.

Year.

With my name next to hers on a certificate.

"The night you were supposed to take me—" she stalled. I gave her time, stroking her arms and tried not to glance back at the doorway, counting mentally in my head and ignoring the stupid damn clock. "That night you, we— everyone. Daddy had people around while I got ready. Men." Her voice cracked.

My arms tightened about her frame. I loosened them with effort. "It's okay, love. I won't leave you, and they can't hurt you now. Looks like your daddy taught you how to protect yourself just fine."

After the fact, maybe, but Grant went up a notch in my estimation.

I leaned back, grabbing for our clothes I collected earlier, and dressed her one-handed as she talked, then myself.

"They came into my room. After their meeting. Something about the school, wanting to limit who attended. Daddy, he didn't like it."

"Bonnie." I kissed her temple. My eyes weren't the only ones on the door. I had a damn good idea where this conversation was headed.

Her tears drenched my arm long before she told me what she kept inside all these years. "I couldn't stop them. Too many. My dress was ripped."

I swallowed. She went shopping for that damn dress with her mother weeks before prom. I remembered I hadn't been allowed to see it. They teased me with the thought of her dressed up and I played along, aching to see her, waiting for her. So damn gorgeous just in jeans and a t-shirt. My girl.

"Fuck, Bonnie." I kissed her mouth before she could keep talking. "Love you."

"Love you, too."

The platitude didn't go far, but she pressed into me as I fixed the back of her dress and managed to wrap my belt around my waist, checking for my wallet, my badge I'd need the moment the local cops rocked up, and a different sort of rock.

"Mom came in halfway through. She saw everything." Bonnie's voice broke in full. "He held down, and she tried to help but they'd, I don't know, someone kept Daddy away. He didn't know, couldn't help. He was heartbroken after. Called the police, reported everything. But they police were—"

She choked, and I filled in the rest of the story because I knew this one by heart. Coldness filled my veins.

"The police were paid off because he owned them, didn't he?" I recited by rote. "My grandfather." Fuck. The one case I'd been after, all these years. If I'd been able to put him away earlier, she'd have been free that much sooner. "This was his man, wasn't he?" I jerked my head back toward the body cooling on the carpet. She nodded, and sucked in a breath. "The reason you haven't been able to come back to Texas at all?" Another nod. "Christ, love. I've failed you. Not being there for you."

"I wasn't allowed to. The police. I– they took me away. I– I asked them to drive past the prom. I saw you that night. You looked so angry."

I stared down at her, horror building in my gut. "I saw that. The police car. I thought it was a routine drive by, checking on the kids. Our safety." I uttered a hollow laugh. You were right fucking there, love. I could have–" I slammed a fist backward into the plaster by the headboard and put my knuckles right through the wall.

Bonnie didn't even flinch, only burrowed deeper into my chest, her tears soaking my shirt, but I didn't care. Her hand slipped through my fingers, trying to pry my hand open, kissing the tiny cuts I put on my own skin.

"Don't hurt yourself. Nash, please, let me hold your hand–"

Her desperate plea snapped off as I opened my fingers, displaying the diamond ring sitting in the middle of my palm.

"I've had this in my pocket ever since that night. I knew it was too early, and it was everything I had saved for a car we talked about me buying that I used on this instead." I caught her hand and as she nodded, her lips parted, I slipped the ring always meant for her onto her finger. Her tears flowed fresh and fast as I kissed her knuckles, folding my bloodied ones over hers. "I love you, Bonnie. I want my name next to yours forever. It's always been us." I searched her eyes. "I wish I'd been there. Would have fought for you. But damn, girl. I'll fight for you now." I hit stop on the recording on my phone, knowing I'd need that later, and pulled her in for a deep kiss when she didn't fight me.

She nodded, but her eyes were serious when I let

her breathe. "What if I'm in jail for the next twenty years for killing a man?"

"That? That was defense, love. I promise." I sent off two messages, one to my local FBI contact, the next to Archer, and pocketed my phone.

That pocket suddenly seemed a hell of a lot lighter. "Wanna tell your daddy before the cops arrive and we gotta tell them everything all over again?"

She kept on nodding, and let me lead her back around the dead man whose name I still didn't know to Grant.

He didn't turn his head when she hugged him, but did hold out an arm. "I heard," he said gruffly. "You sure you want to be hitched to a Texas Ranger, Bon-Bon?"

She glanced at me with wide eyes. "Is that what you are?"

I shrugged. "It's new to me, too. I was FBI."

"Oh." She blinked at me. "Daddy? We're getting married in Texas."

He looked down at her and ignored me. "You trust him?"

"We always should have."

My heart glowed in my chest as she released her father and slipped her arms around my waist.

Then, we waited.

Epilogue

BONNIE

Three days after Christmas, most of which we spent in a very prettily decorated police station at Love Beach, Nash drove us across the country back to Texas. I stood at the border of the land I last saw a decade and change ago, wondering if I was actually allowed to step foot onto my native home.

Mom and Dad were taking their time coming back, and I didn't think it was all about Mom, though Dad insisted it was. Part of me wondered how much he didn't want to see Texas again, either. Nash offered his own home open to us while we found our feet again, and his Texas Rangers provided protection for my entire family, and me.

It was like they adopted us the moment his case blew open, though I knew he hadn't been part of them for very long either. A new family for all. Merry Christmas, bordering on a new year.

Even a happy one.

Part of me still struggled with the fact I killed a man, thanks to Daddy teaching me years ago how to handle a gun until the guise of taking me hunting as a kid and swapping out my rifle on occasion for a handgun I suspected he stole from somewhere.

That was back in the early days when he seemed to think we might escape from our hideous life moving from place to place under the watchful eye of Texas' worst and most dreadful.

They didn't seem to want to pull the trigger on our strange impasse, and we ended up in an endless bout of self-inflicted purgatory. I think they were waiting for us to implode, but that never happened thanks to Daddy's deep, deep pockets.

Now, that long, stagnant stage of my life was over. A full third, and I was free thanks to Nash's quick talking to the local police and his connections with law enforcement.

Which brought us, quite literally, back to Texas.

"Bonnie," Nash said my name like a caress. He

stood with his hand outstretched, him on the other side of that state line. After this we'd still have a long way to go to get to his home, but right here, this moment—it meant so much to both of us.

My heart lived on that land, with him. But my feet flat out refused to move.

"How did you do it?" I pleaded, locking my fingers together into a knot. "When you were called back."

Nash considered me for a long moment before he answered. "I wanted answers. I wanted that case to close up with my grandfather. My mother hadn't seen me in years, and I didn't call because I pushed her and everyone else away." He took a step closer until we were toe to toe with an invisible line dividing us, a breath wide. "But most of all, I wanted to find you."

My eyes shuttered, tears dropping with them. One day I'd stop crying, but today the tears still fell. One day. Maybe.

I reached out and he lifted me off my feet, turning us in a circle and placed me on Texas land.

My feet didn't move. Heat ran up my ankles, but the ground didn't shake, and the world didn't end.

"How does it feel to be home, love?"

I smiled into his shirt, breathed in his leather and whiskey and caramel scent, ran my fingers over the star badge he displayed on his belt, and smiled.

"Like I'm supposed to be here with you."

Read more Nash and Bonnie

(and that bleacher fantasy he detailed back at the resort)

in their BONUS EPILOGUE FOR FREE

Thank you for reading MERRY WITH A RANGER! Nash and Bonnie's story turned out to have a hugely more emotional punch than I expected (hey, it happens!) and thank you so much for sticking with us to the end. Please do leave a review. I appreciate and read every single one.

What to read next:

Following on with TEXAN DEVILS after Nash...

SUMMER WITH A RANGER (HUDSON)
Snapdragons & Seductions (Acton)

TEXAN DEVILS
RANGER'S WISH
RANGER BEDEVILLED
RANGER'S PASSION
RANGER'S FURY
RANGER'S WRATH
RANGER'S DILEMMA
RANGER'S STORM

RED HART RANCH (crossover series)
SNOW ON THE RANGE
SIREN ON THE RANGE
SUNDOWN ON THE RANGE
SHADOW ON THE RANGE
SPIRIT ON THE RANGE

About the Author

USA Today Bestselling author Sofia Aves writes fast-paced police romances, sizzling military units, steamy cowboys with a Montana backdrop and the occasional cheeky god. Married to a veteran, she often tackles topics of PTSD and reintegration and has a soft spot for all who work in uniform. Sofia writes kidlit for charity and has over one hundred and fifty publications across four not-so-super-secret pen names.

Publishing is her life. She has been a marketing manager for both Romance Writers of Australia, and Romance Cafe Publishing and an acquisitions editor for Evernight and Evernight Teen. Sofia is a mum of three crazies in a returned veteran household and has an overly large fur baby who thinks she's a teacup puppy. Sofia lives near Brisbane, Australia where she runs her alpaca park, Lorendel.

Read Sofia's Series

Blue **Blooded Brothers** *Police romance*

Collision

Politics & Paperwork

Blindsided

Sentinel

Mugshots & Candy Canes

Impact

Reckoning

Red Hart Ranch *Cowboy Romance*

Snow on the Range

Siren on the Range

Sundown on the Range

Spirit on the Range

Ash on the Range

Mistletoe on the Range

Forgotten Mountain Man

<u>Forsaken Mountain Man</u>

Texan Devils Romantic Suspense

Ranger's Wish

Ranger Bedevilled

Ranger's Passion

Ranger's Fury

Ranger's Wrath

Ranger's Storm

Snapdragons & Seductions

Summer with a Ranger

Merry with a Ranger

Playing to Win Sports Romance

Off Boarding

Vicious Slash

Zero Pointer

Off Stage Fling

.   .   .

Rippton Allstars Hockey Dark Romance

Crushing It

Glacial Force

Rippton Creatives Dark Romance

Study Games

Make Me, Break Me

Twisted Obsession

Spring Break with a Mafia Prince

A Royally Fake French Menage

Angel Shot

Jericho Chimeras Hockey Romance

Puck Me Always

Puck My Heart

Puck me Sideways

Z Boys Military Romance

King

Joker

Hearts

Ace

Mayhem & Mistletoe

Ruski

Fast Track to Love *Racing Romance*
Speed Trap

Klauss Brothers *Christmas Short Romance*
Zander
Keegan
Gallo Mafia Empire *with Jade Marshall*
Splintered Vows
Fractured Vows
Fierce Vows
Savage Covenant

Christmas Standalone Rom Coms
She's A Hot Christmas Mess
Boats, Moats and Root Beer Floats

Writing Romantasy as
SOFIA SHELLEY
Dead Poets Sorority

. . .

Writing spicy Paranormal romance as

RAVEN HUSH

Club Fray

Darkest Desires

Purge

Kidnapped By Claws

Ruin

Shadow Lords

Sinner's End

Heaven's Gate (2026)

Monster Brides

Phoenix's Eternal Flame

Kraken's Vow

Krampus' Christmas Bride

Silent Sentinels Duet

Reflections of Silence

Echoes in the Void

. . .

Monsters In New York
　　Feral Moon Rising
　　Dark Water Refuge

Writing Reverse Harem Dark Romance as
　　DOVE PRIEST
　　Recurve Ridge

Writing kidlit as
　　JO SEYSENER
　　The OCD Elf
　　The OCD Elf's Great Reindeer Calamity
　　Greg and the Egg

writing YA as
　　JOSS PHOENIX
　　Alchem Academy
　　HIDE FROM US

www.ingramcontent.com/pod-product-compliance
Lightning Source LLC
Chambersburg PA
CBHW060221030726
47499CB00004B/1139